Alison Roberts is a New Zealander, currently lucky enough to be living in the South of France. She is also lucky enough to write for the Mills & Boon Medical Romance line. A primary school teacher in a former life, she is now a qualified paramedic. She loves to travel and dance, drink champagne, and spend time with her daughter and her friends.

SINGLE DAD IN HER STOCKING

ALISON ROBERTS

MILLS & BOON

First published in Great Britain 2019
by Mills & Boon, an imprint of HarperCollins*Publishers*
1 London Bridge Street, London, SE1 9GF

Large Print edition 2020

© 2019 Alison Roberts

ISBN: 978-0-263-08564-8

MIX
Paper from
responsible sources
FSC **FSC C007454**

This book is produced from independently certified
FSC™ paper to ensure responsible forest management. For
more information visit www.harpercollins.co.uk/green.

Printed and bound in Great Britain
by CPI Group (UK) Ltd, Croydon, CR0 4YY

CHAPTER ONE

'OH, NO…YOU can't be serious.'

'I'm so sorry, Dr Cunningham, but there it is. I'm sure you understand that acute appendicitis isn't something we can plan for. We're doing our very best to find someone else to fill the position but, realistically, that's not going to happen until after New Year. People want to be with their families over the festive season and…it's such late notice. It's the twentieth of December, for heaven's sake. Christmas is only a few days away, you know.'

Of course he knew. There was tinsel in all sorts of odd places in his emergency department here at the Cheltenham Royal Hospital and there was a small Christmas tree in the waiting room. Some staff members had taken to wearing earrings that had flashing lights or headbands with reindeer antlers or little red hats with pompoms attached and he kept hearing people humming Christmas carols. They'd even had a man in a Santa suit come in by ambulance earlier today after suffering a suspected heart attack as he coped with all those small people wanting to sit on his knee and have their photographs taken in the town's largest department store.

And, of course, he knew that people wanted to be with their families. Or felt obliged to be. It was precisely the reason why Max Cunningham always worked right through the holiday season to make sure as many people as possible in his department could have time at home with their loved ones. He'd done it for so many years now he was quite comfortable ignoring the commercial hype that tried to make it compulsory for happy families to gather and have an over-the-top celebration as they enjoyed each other's company. It was as much of a myth as Santa Claus as far as he was concerned—or it was for the Cunningham family, at any rate.

Everybody knew that. He could just imagine how much of a field day any gossips of Upper Barnsley would have when the news of a third December tragedy to hit the Cunningham family filtered out. Talk about history repeating itself.

It's struck again, they'd probably say. *The Christmas Curse of the Cunninghams...*

He'd been too young to do anything but cope the first time when his mother had died. Last time had been gutting when he'd lost his only brother but he'd got through it. Somehow. Life had gone back to normal. But this year was different. This year, his entire world was being tipped upside down and the phone call he'd just taken meant that Max could expect even more disruption. So much more, he wasn't at all sure he knew what to do about it and feeling less than confident was as new and uncomfortable a sensation as any of the changes that were about to happen in his life. Nothing was ever going to go back to normal now, was it?

'Hey…it can't be that bad.' The Royal's senior nurse in the emergency department, Miriam, came into Max's office. 'Here, have a chocolate. I thought I'd bring you one before they all got scoffed by those gannets in the staffroom. Look, how cute are these? Like little plum puddings.'

Max shook his head. 'No, thanks. I'm not really in the mood for chocolate. I've got a bit of a problem, to be honest.'

Miriam's face creased in sympathy. 'I did hear that something was going on. To do with your brother? And his children...?'

'My brother Andy died just over a year ago. A car accident.' It was a testament to how Max managed to keep his private life private that nobody here was aware of the full story but Miriam was trustworthy—the kind of motherly type that inspired confidence from both her patients and her colleagues. A great listener, too, with enough life experience to offer sage advice in almost any situation. Max could do with some advice.

'It was his wife, this time,' he added. 'Or, I should say, his ex-wife. I haven't seen his children since his funeral. I didn't even know that there was a third one.'

'Oh?' Miriam's eyebrows rose as she sank

into the chair in front of Max's desk. 'Why ever not?'

Max sighed. 'His marriage had broken down and he was dealing with difficult custody issues. He didn't know that his wife was pregnant when she left and she obviously wasn't too keen to keep in touch with the rest of his family after he died. She moved all the way up to somewhere north of Glasgow.'

'And she's the one who's just died?'

'Yes. She was taking the oldest one to school. Ben. He's six. Icy road and an elderly driver must have panicked when he went into a skid and put his foot down on the accelerator. She managed to shove the baby's pushchair out of the way but got killed instantly herself. There was an elderly aunt or someone who made funeral arrangements but she couldn't take care of the children. They were all put into foster care while they tried to track down any other family.'

'And you're the children's guardian?'

'So it would seem. Maybe it was a legal document that got overlooked in the separation and then Andy died so a formal divorce never happened. It's a good thing. It would have been appalling if Andy's kids had been left in foster care when they've got an uncle and grandfather who are quite willing and able to take care of them.'

Well…being willing was one thing. Being able could prove to be a lot harder.

'Your dad's the GP in Upper Barnsley, isn't he?'

'Yes. And he lives in a house that's ridiculously big for one person, but the house has been in the family for generations and he says the only way he's leaving it is feet first when they carry out his dead body.' Max found a smile. 'That's also a good thing because there's plenty of room for the children. His housekeeper is happy to help out a bit more than doing her usual weekly shop and clean and I'd made arrangements for a live-in nanny who was going to get here tomorrow, in time for when the children arrive.'

'Sounds like you've got things well under control.'

Max rubbed at his jaw. 'I thought I had. But I've just had a call from the agency and the nanny got rushed into hospital a couple of hours ago with acute appendicitis. She's probably on an operating table as we speak… and they have no one else available until after New Year.'

'Oh…no…' Miriam's despairing tone was an exact echo of the one he'd used on receiving that news. 'I wish I could offer to help but I've got family coming from all over the country this year. Christmas dinner for fourteen people and I've only got one day off to do the rest of the grocery shopping. It's going to be a bit of a nightmare.' But the older woman's smile suggested that she was rather looking forward to the chaos.

'I do have an idea, though,' she added a moment later.

Max was open to any ideas because he had none of his own. He could even feel an edge of panic hovering—as if he was about to go into a skid that he wouldn't be able to control—like the unfortunate one that had killed his ex-sister-in-law a few weeks ago. Who was going to get injured by this one? Himself or his father? His nieces or nephew? He was about to become the father figure to children who had suffered unimaginable loss of both their parents and their home. Their whole world. Was he about to stumble at the first hurdle of this new journey? No…he couldn't allow that to happen.

'What's your idea?' he asked.

'There's an agency we've used before. London Locums. They're a specialist medical recruitment agency and they might be worth a try even with such short notice and at such a difficult time of the year. I could ring them if you like?'

'But I need a nanny, not a locum doctor.'

Miriam's smile was gentle. 'Don't you think it would be better for those poor children to have family looking after them instead of strangers? Why not get a locum to cover *you*? That way, you could be with the children to help them settle in. They must be so scared by all the changes happening around them.'

Max swallowed hard. He was a bit scared himself, to be honest. It wasn't that he didn't like children. He had enjoyed being an uncle and welcoming his brother's first two children into the world and he got on very well with the small people who came through the doors of his emergency department. He just hadn't ever planned to have any of his own.

Ever.

The disintegration of his own happiness when he was a child, after losing his mother—the sun of their family universe—had left an indelible stain. He had watched his father grapple with a sadness that meant he had no resources to provide for the emotional needs of two young boys and it had been Max who had tried to help his younger brother. That the sadness had morphed into a lasting depression that his father would never admit to or seek help for had cemented the deeply absorbed knowledge that the fallout of a family breaking apart for whatever reason was simply not worth the risk.

Max Cunningham had finally discovered the delicious balance of his passion for working hard and as brilliantly as possible with playing just as hard outside of work hours and that time almost always included a beautiful woman as a playmate. Max was confident that he had honed his skills in making a woman feel very, very special but only for a limited amount of time, of course. He wasn't ever going to get caught in the trap of having his happiness depend on a family, only to have his world destroyed. If his own childhood memories hadn't been enough, his brother's death last year had more than re-inforced his belief that the risk was far too great. He hadn't ever intended to be respon-sible for the happiness of others either, by try-ing to create and protect the safety of a family unit or to patch up the fragments of a world that had been irreparably broken.

But, here he was, about to attempt exactly that and the responsibilities about to land on his doorstep were more than daunting. Who knew how traumatised these children already were? The girls might be too young to re-member losing their father last year but little Ben was six and maybe he was already try-ing to wear the mantle of the oldest child and look after his siblings and Max knew how hard that could be. And Miriam was right. The children had been in the care of total strangers since they'd lost their mother and that wasn't acceptable. Max might think his world was being upended but for his nephew and nieces the only world they knew had just vanished for ever.

'And it's *Christmas*,' Miriam added softly, as she got to her feet—as if that settled the matter. 'They're family. And they need you.'

'Emma?'

'Hi, Julie.' Emma Moretti paused beneath the bare branches of trees in London's Hyde Park as she answered her phone, watching a squirrel race up the trunk of the nearest tree. 'I hope you've got some good news for me?'

Julie was the manager of London Locums, the specialist medical recruitment agency that Emma had been employed by for the last few years.

'You're not going to believe it. After telling you there was absolutely nothing on the books for the Christmas period, I just got a call from someone at the Royal in Cheltenham. They're desperate for someone to take over from their emergency department HOD.

Seems he's got some family crisis happening until some time in early January.'

'ED? My favourite.' Emma's outward breath was almost a sigh of relief. She was desperate to get out of London for a few days. At least until Christmas was over. There were too many memories here and it felt harder this year, for some reason. Maybe she hadn't got past things as well as she thought she had. Or maybe it was because, at thirty-six, her last birthday had reminded her that the window of opportunity for having the family she'd always dreamt of was beginning to close. Worse, she still wasn't sure she was ready to do something proactive about that. Even after nearly five years, she hadn't ever given serious thought to changing her single status.

'Are you sure, Em? I don't think the Royal really expects us to be able to provide someone at such short notice and you know how crazy emergency departments can get over Christmas. People drink far too much and there's all those weird accidents you hear about, like people falling off the roof because they're trying to change the bulb on Rudolph's nose or something. You could just go on holiday if you wanted to escape. Somewhere nice and warm like the Maldives. Or Australia? Goodness knows you've earned a break and they're talking snow here. Possibly a white Christmas for once.'

Going on holiday alone would be the worst thing to do. It would give her far too much time to think. To remember things that were better left in the past.

'You know me,' she reminded Julie. 'I kind of like crazy.'

'What about Italy, then?' Julie was a good friend as well as her employer. 'When did you last have Christmas with *your* family?'

A long time ago. But not quite long enough, it would seem, because she still wasn't ready for a full-on Italian-style family gathering. Or perhaps it had just become a habit because locums were always in such demand over holiday periods.

'Are you kidding?' Emma tried to keep her tone light. 'My cousin has just had twins. My mother will be crying in the corner because her only child is thirty-six and still single and maybe she'll never get any grandchildren of her own. They'll probably drag in every eligible male in the village and try and arrange a marriage on the spot. You have no idea the kind of pressure that will entail.' She managed a laugh. 'Give me medical chaos any time. Please, I need to be in Cheltenham. My family won't mind. They know I always work over Christmas.'

'Well…if you're sure. It does have accommodation on offer as well. A modern apartment near the hospital. Let me see…a suburb called Montpellier.'

'Sounds French. *Trés chic.*' Emma drew in a deep breath. 'It's perfect, Julie. When do I need to be there?'

'Early tomorrow afternoon by the latest. Someone called Miriam will give you an orientation tour and supply the keys to the apartment. I'll text you the details.'

It was no more than a brisk walk to the compact basement apartment where Emma lived alone. It wouldn't take her long to pack. She'd been with London Locums long enough to know exactly what she needed to take and to be ready to leave the city at a moment's notice if necessary. It had been a huge life-style change to leave her secure position as a junior consultant in a paediatric ward, but it had been the perfect choice at the time. There was an adrenaline rush to be found, never knowing what kind of job would be around the next corner. She could be taking over a general practice in a remote area to give a sole GP a proper holiday, doing aero-medical retrievals from some exotic location with a seriously ill or injured person who needed to come home or plugging a gap in a hospital roster like this time. And an emergency department really was her favourite place to work—maybe because it was a bit like her lifestyle. You got to do all sorts of exciting, satisfying things but only for a brief time. Patients got moved on to other departments. She got to move on to other positions and that was the way she liked it.

If you never put down roots or formed deep attachments, there was no danger of having the pain of them getting ripped out, was there? Life was so much easier this way.

A busker, just outside the park gates, was—predictably—singing a Christmas carol. Emma increased her pace as she tried to escape the lyrics of 'Mary's Boy Child' because it never failed to bring tears to her eyes every time. Just those four words—*born on Christmas Day*—could still potentially rip a hole in her heart.

It was five years ago now, though. She would have expected it to be getting easier year by year and it was…except for Christmas. Sometimes it felt as if the whole world was conspiring to remind her in agonising detail of how hard it had been to have coped as well as she had. Especially being here, because the hospital where it had happened—and where she'd worked at the time—was just on the other side of the park.

Thank goodness she could head out of town first thing tomorrow.

Emma couldn't wait. She made a mental note to make sure she had some chains in the back of her SUV. Just in case. A town as big as Cheltenham was highly unlikely to get snowed in but it was surrounded by winding country roads and isolated villages. A white Christmas with all the extra chaos that could bring to an emergency department?

Bring it on...

'She's here, Max. With an apology for being a bit late but she said the traffic on the M40 was diabolical. There'd been a crash.'

'No problem. At least she's here now. Thanks, Miriam. Can you give her a really quick tour of the department to get her up to speed to start her first shift tomorrow morning and then bring her in here? I've got a couple of things I must finish but then I'll be heading off to Upper Barnsley. I'll need to be there when the children arrive.'

'Of course. You'll be wanting to give her the keys and any instructions for your apartment?'

'I think it would be polite to actually show her the apartment myself. It's only a few minutes' walk away, after all. It's not going to hold me up. Oh…' Max lifted an eyebrow. 'What's her name?'

'Emma…something. Sounded Italian but I can't remember. She looks competent, though.' Miriam's mouth twitched. 'I'm sure you'll approve.'

Max cringed just a little at the inference he couldn't miss. Yes, he appreciated good-looking women and there never seemed to be a shortage of contenders to fill the inevitably changing position as his out-of-work-hours companion but there was something in his senior nurse's expression that made him think his reputation might not be something to be proud of. Well, it was irrelevant now, anyway. Even if he had any opportunities to meet someone new in the foreseeable future, he wouldn't be able to take advantage of them. He had other, far more pressing, responsibilities that were due to land on his doorstep in—he swallowed hard as he glanced at his watch—only a hour or two from now.

He turned his attention back to the computer screen in front of him. There were a few last-minute adjustments to make to the rosters to ensure that this department ran as smoothly as possible while he couldn't be here. He needed to give this Emma his personal mobile number as well so he could be on call to give her any advice if she needed it.

An Emma with an Italian-sounding surname was ringing a vague bell in the back of his mind as he pulled up a spreadsheet. It came with an image of a laughing young woman surrounded by children, holding a baby that had his hands tangled in her long ponytail. A quintessential 'earth mother' type, which, of course, had made her an absolute 'no-go' type for Max—no matter how gorgeous those generous curves and dark eyes and that smile had been.

Good grief...that had been ten years ago but the memory was astonishingly clear, now that he had dredged it up. They'd both been junior doctors on a paediatric ward at the same time. And her name was Emma...dammit... what had her surname been?

'Moretti.'

Max's gaze flicked up to the figure standing in the doorway of his office. He'd been totally lost in thought and the fact that the answer to his internal query was being answered in person had just thrown him completely.

'I'm Emma Moretti,' she said, coming further into the small space. 'Miriam said to pop in and see you?'

Was it really the same woman? This Emma Moretti was nothing like the one Max had just been remembering. She was slim and smartly dressed and had short, spiky dark hair like a brunette pixie. She wasn't smiling but her eyes were certainly dark enough. Almost as black as her hair. And she was staring at him with just the same astonished intensity that he knew he was subjecting her to.

'*Max?* No way...' Her lips were curving into a smile now and, suddenly, Max could see the woman he remembered. The life and soul of any party, especially if there were children involved. And that thought led straight to another party he couldn't help but remember. The Christmas function for the staff of that paediatric ward. That sprig of mistletoe he'd held over Emma's head. That kiss... The way they'd both laughed and blamed it on the prosecco because they couldn't have been more wrong for each other.

Emma was still smiling. 'I knew the HOD was a Dr Cunningham, but I never for a moment thought it might be you. I would have imagined you to be living in a place like New York by now. Or Sydney, maybe.'

A large, vibrant city that would be a perfect social playground for someone with a reputation like himself? That cringeworthy moment he'd had earlier came back to bite a little harder. Ten years on and he hadn't changed much, had he?

Unlike Emma.

'And I would never have imagined you working as a locum. I would have imagined you to be completely settled in one place by now. With a husband and half a dozen kids.'

He was genuinely curious about what had happened in her life but he knew he'd just stepped over a boundary of some kind. He saw the instant the shutters went up.

'Nobody has half a dozen kids these days,

Max. How irresponsible would that be, given global resources?'

Max cleared his throat. 'Precisely why I haven't contributed to the population statistics myself.' He shuffled some papers on his desk to cover the slightly awkward atmosphere. 'Did Miriam give you enough of a tour? Are you happy to start your first shift at seven a.m. tomorrow?'

'I'm happy.' Emma's nod was brisk. 'I've had a lot of experience working in unfamiliar surroundings and I can quickly get a feel for how helpful the staff are going to be. You've obviously got a great crowd here and I don't anticipate any problems at all in covering for you. I assume you have a trauma team on call as well? With specialists from other departments?'

'Yes. I can't guarantee there'll be a consultant from every department available on the bank holidays but there should be someone from orthopaedics, general surgery and neurology who'll get here as fast as possible if the alert is activated. We only do that if we know there's major trauma coming in. Otherwise, we assess and call in consults as needed. Same goes for medical or obstetric emergencies.' Max closed down his computer and got to his feet. 'I'll be available by phone at any time. Don't hesitate to call. I can probably come in if there's a real crisis. I'll be just outside of a village that's halfway between Cheltenham and Cirencester, which is only twenty minutes away—unless this forecast for snow is accurate.'

'I'm rather hoping for a white Christmas,' Emma said. 'Especially seeing as I've got accommodation that's within easy walking distance.'

'Speaking of which…let's go.' Max headed towards Emma to reach for his coat that was hanging behind the door. He caught a faint scent of something clean and crisp as he got closer. Lemons, maybe? Or mandarins…?

'Sorry?' Emma was blinking at him. 'Where are we going?'

'To the apartment.' Max held open the door of his office. 'I thought I'd show you around, seeing as it's mine.'

* * *

The HOD of the Royal's emergency department was making his own apartment available for his locum?

And the HOD was Max Cunningham?

Emma was still getting her head around both of these startling pieces of information as she followed him out of the emergency department via the automatic doors that led to the ambulance bay.

It would probably be a swanky penthouse apartment, she decided. Very modern and luxurious and not at all to her taste but perfect for a brief stay. Unless…oh, help…could there be something really tacky like mirrors on the bedroom ceiling?

Everybody had known what Max Cunningham was like back in the day of their junior rotations. Not that that stopped women from joining the queue. And why not? Max was drop-dead gorgeous, totally charming and knew how to make any woman feel special. He'd had a catchphrase, hadn't he?

Oh, yeah… Emma bit back a smile as they turned out from the hospital grounds and waited for a set of traffic lights to change so that they could cross the busy main road. She remembered it now.

We're here for a good time, not a long time...

Playboys had never been remotely Emma's type but she had understood the attraction. Felt it herself, in fact, even though she wouldn't have touched him with a bargepole as far as a relationship went. The man had actually kissed *her* once, at that Christmas party and...and...good grief... How was it possible to remember a moment like that with such astonishing detail after so many years? She could feel her toes trying to curl themselves up inside her shoes so it was a relief to start walking swiftly across the road. She certainly wasn't going to start wondering if the toe-curling was due to embarrassment or the intense desire that kiss had generated. There were decorations overhead, she noticed, trying to distract herself further by looking up. Long strings of icicle lights that would look very pretty at night.

'Five minutes' walk, that's all,' Max was

saying. 'And the place should be perfectly clean. My housekeeper went in a few days ago and gave it a thorough going-over and changed the linen and so on. I'll make sure you have her number as well, in case you need anything else.'

'That's great. Thank you very much. I usually end up in a hotel or something when I'm doing a short locum like this.'

'We did think of that, but a quick check told us that there was nothing available. For some reason, Cheltenham seems like a very popular destination for the festive season.'

'No room at the inns, then?' Emma caught Max's sideways glance. 'Quite appropriate, really.'

His smile hadn't changed at all. Or the way the corners of his eyes crinkled to make his appreciation appear completely genuine. Ten years had given him a few grey hairs and deepened those lines a bit but, if anything, they had just made Max even more attractive.

'Here we are...' Max keyed a code into the front door of a very modern building and led the way to an elevator. He pushed a button that wasn't the top floor.

'Not the penthouse?' Emma murmured. 'You surprise me, Max.'

He shook his head. 'Was I really that much of a plonker in those days?'

'Not at all. From what I remember you were a brilliant doctor. You just had a reputation for playing as hard as you worked, I guess.'

'Those days are over.' He didn't sound too happy about that, Emma thought, but he wasn't about to tell her why. 'The penthouse here is very nice, I believe,' he added. 'But it's empty most of the time. The guy who owns it is something high up in a bank and has to travel a lot.'

Emma followed him out of the elevator. She watched as he unlocked the door but then her gaze dropped.

'What's that?'

'What?'

'All that water.'

The carpet outside the door was soaked. As Max lifted his foot, his shoe was dripping. 'Oh, *no*...' He pushed the door open and stepped in. The tiled entranceway to his apartment shimmered like a small lake. 'Stay there,' he warned Emma. 'This doesn't look good.'

But she followed him in, looking over his shoulder as he checked a bathroom to see whether taps had been left on. There was a bedroom that had water dripping from the bulb in the ceiling light.

'It's coming from upstairs,' Max muttered. 'A burst pipe, perhaps…' He sighed. 'I've been staying with my father for the last few days or I might have noticed this happening soon enough to prevent this much damage.'

So that was the family crisis? His father being ill? He certainly didn't need this complication on top of other worries. Emma felt very sorry for Max but it was very clear that she wasn't going to be able to stay here. It was the main living room that was the real disaster. Enough water had seeped into the ceiling to make the plasterwork too heavy. Large sections had fallen to cover the couches and a glass-topped coffee table.

To give him credit, Max was very calm as

he took control of the situation. 'I'll have to call the building manager,' he said. 'Give me a minute.'

As soon as he'd made the call, he turned back to Emma. 'You can't stay here, obviously,' he said. 'We'll find a hotel nearby—there'll probably be somewhere we overlooked before. I'll pay for it.' He was focused on his phone again. 'Let's just see what's available on one of those comparison sites.'

Emma had taken out her own phone. A minute or two of silence and then they both looked up.

'Not looking good, is it?' Emma said. 'As soon as I put the dates in there's no availability at all.'

'There'll be something.' Max was obviously trying to sound reassuring. 'We might have to look a bit further afield, that's all.' He hesitated, glancing at his watch. 'That could take a bit of time but don't worry, I'm not going to leave you in the lurch. You can come with me for the moment. As I said, the place I'm staying is only twenty minutes away so, even if we can't find you a suitable hotel room to-

night, it won't be a difficult commute tomorrow morning unless the weather turns nasty.'

'I've got chains,' she told him. 'But…this
is your father's house you're talking about,
yes?' A hotel room would be preferable. Perhaps Emma should just stay in town and keep
trying to find something.

'He'll be just as concerned as I am that my
locum is well looked after,' Max said. 'It's a
big house and there's more than enough room
for visitors. It was probably built to cater for
a Victorian couple who had twelve children.'
He gestured for Emma to lead the way out
of the apartment. 'They weren't so worried
about global resources in those days.'

He might be making a joke but a glance at
his face suggested to Emma that the hypo-
thetical camel's back might have just been
loaded with the last straw.

'I should keep trying to find a hotel,' she
said. 'I wouldn't want to intrude. Not if your
father is so unwell.'

'Unwell?' Max's eyebrows rose. 'He's as
fit as a fiddle.' He looked at his watch again
and stifled a groan. 'Come on, you'll have to

follow me to Upper Barnsley in your car. We don't have that much time before the children arrive.'

Children?

But hadn't Max said that he hadn't personally contributed to the population statistics? Emma was curious but the look of fierce concentration on Max's face was enough to stop her asking any more questions as they hurried back to the hospital car park. Besides, the mention of children had reminded her of that assumption he'd voiced—that she would have a husband and a tribe of children by now— and there was a sting in that assumption that needed to be dealt with. Back in those days, she had assumed exactly the same thing so it was no wonder he was surprised. She had been more than surprised herself, of course. Having her life derailed like that had been devastating but at least she was well past the toughest time of her life, when working only with children and babies as a specialist paediatrician had proved hard enough to have dimmed the joy and she'd been tempted to change the direction she had chosen for her career. She could cope with children.

As long as she didn't get too close to them...

Life had a habit of upending plans sometimes and it appeared that it was happening again, Emma decided, as she followed Max out of town and into the pretty countryside of the Cotswolds with its narrow roads and tiny villages full of trees and stone-built cottages. Her most recent plans had already gone more than a little awry, with her accommodation proving uninhabitable. The person she was replacing was unexpectedly someone she had once been more than a little attracted to, even though she would never have gone there, and she was now being whisked away to some unknown but large house by this still very attractive man and there were children involved, which didn't make any sense at all. Unless Max had acquired an instant family by marrying someone who already had children? Or this house with far too many bedrooms was being run as some kind of foster home or orphanage?

She hadn't even started her new locum

position and they still had several days before Christmas arrived but it seemed like the chaos had already begun. As a few fat flakes of snow drifted gently onto her windscreen, Emma found she was smiling wryly.

Almost grinning a few moments later, in fact.

She had needed a distraction and it would appear that the universe was providing one.

CHAPTER TWO

UPPER BARNSLEY WAS bigger than other villages they had driven through, with its high street full of shops, a village green and a market square with a tall Christmas tree as a centrepiece. Moments later, Emma was following Max's vehicle down a long, tree-lined driveway to stop in front of a house that took her breath away. She was still blinking up at the huge, three-storeyed gabled mansion with imposing chimneys and ivy creeping up its stone walls as Max opened the heavy wooden front door and waited for her to go inside.

'You grew up here?' Somehow it didn't fit with the image of the contemporary 'man about town' she'd met in that London paediatric ward a decade ago. She gazed from one side of the entranceway to the other. There was probably a library in here. And a drawing room like they had in those period dramas on television with dogs lying in front of an open fire big enough to roast an ox. 'This is amazing.'

Max simply nodded. 'It's been in the family for more than a hundred years. Known locally as Cunningham Manor.' He raised his voice. 'Dad? You here?'

A woman who looked to be in her late fifties appeared from a doorway at the far end of the entrance foyer. 'He's in the west wing,' she told Max. 'Oh…who's this?' She was wiping her hands on her apron and beaming as she came towards Emma. 'I'm Maggie—Dr Cunningham's housekeeper. Dr Cunningham senior, that is,' she added.

Max took pity on her. 'The west wing is a private joke. Dad's the GP for Upper Barnsley and the lower level of that side of the house used to be the stables, I believe. It was converted to be a clinic years before I was born.' He turned to the housekeeper. 'This is Emma Moretti,' he told her. 'She's the locum who's taking over from me at the hospital until we get the nanny situation sorted. She also happens to be an old friend of mine. We worked together in a paediatric ward a very long time ago.'

Emma wasn't about to contradict him publicly but calling her a friend was stretching things a little. They had been colleagues and she'd totally respected his abilities as a doctor but she'd never trusted him enough to think of him as a friend. Or maybe she hadn't trusted herself? If they'd got close, she might have given in to that major attraction she'd felt for Max and how embarrassing could that have been? It had only taken one kiss for him to laugh about how she was 'so not his type'. She'd agreed, of course, and laughed along with him. How else would one save face at a time like that? Besides, he'd been right. He was 'so not her type' as well, but it had been a bit of a put-down to find out that the attraction hadn't actually been mutual.

'Oh...wonderful.' Maggie was still smiling. 'You'll need all the expert help you can get with these babies.'

Babies? A chill ran down Emma's spine. Max had said children, not babies.

Children were so much easier to be around than babies. Especially newborn babies. She could work with them, of course, but preferably in a clinical setting rather than, say, an accident scene. And never in a private home. Even in a medical situation, being present at a birth or close to a tiny baby made the scars on her own heart ache. She might have built barriers to protect herself enough to live with the pain of only ever having a few hours with her own precious baby but she had no desire to deliberately test how strong those protective walls might be.

'I didn't bring Emma here to stand in for the nanny,' Max told Maggie. 'She's supposed to be using my apartment but there's been a small catastrophe with an upstairs flood and she needs to stay here until we can sort that out.'

'It's okay.' Emma found her voice. 'I'm sure I can find somewhere in town. It sounds like you're going to be very busy if…if you're expecting…babies?'

What on earth was going on? she wondered. Was Max sharing custody for step-children of a failed marriage? Had he married someone who had already been pregnant with twins, perhaps? Or triplets? The thought of multiple newborn babies made Emma want to head straight out of the door and keep on going. She even looked in that direction, only to find a broad-shouldered older man coming in through the front door, with a small, scruffy white dog at his heels. It was a vision of what Max would look like in about thirty years' time, she realised. Except that this man didn't have the same charming smile. If anything, he was glowering at Emma.

'What's going on? Who's this? A new nanny?' He shut the door, turned and made an irritated sound. 'Pirate, come here.'

But the small, scruffy dog had made a beeline for Emma, was sitting at her feet and staring up at her with black button eyes. She guessed that he was mostly a West Highland White terrier but it was easy to see where his name had come from because he had a black patch covering one eye and ear. He was very cute. And he was wagging his tail. It was impossible not to bend down and offer him her hand. The small black nose felt cold and damp as it touched her skin.

'Look at that,' Max said. 'That doesn't happen very often. Pirate likes you. And no,' he told his father. 'This is Emma, who's going to be my locum at the Royal. I told you about that plan.'

'I thought she was staying at your place.'

'My place is wrecked. I'll explain later. The kids are due to arrive any minute. Maggie, could I ask you to make up another bedroom for Emma for tonight, at least? It seems that there aren't any hotel rooms to be easily found.'

'No, really... I should go.' Emma actually took a step towards the door. 'If I can't find a hotel room in Cheltenham, I could try Gloucester...?'

'Nonsense.' Maggie's hand was on Emma's elbow. 'We've got ten bedrooms here and I got an extra one ready in case the children wanted their own rooms later but I'm sure they'll want to be together at least for now. Come with me.'

So they were children now? Emma was becoming increasingly confused.

'It's snowing out there,' Max's father said, coming towards her. 'You don't want to be going anywhere if you don't have to. You might get stuck until they come to clear the lanes. I'm James, by the way. James Cunningham. Max seems to have forgotten his manners.'

Max shrugged and offered Emma a crooked smile but there were frown lines on his forehead. And some kind of plea in those dark eyes? The tension in the air here was palpable and Emma suddenly felt trapped but she couldn't run away if someone needed help, could she?

'And you're most welcome to stay,' James continued. Yes, there was a hint of the same kind of smile that Emma remembered his son using to devastating effect. Even a short-lived twinkle in his eyes. 'Pirate is a very good judge of character.' He snapped his fingers at the dog, who instantly went back to his master. 'I'm going to make sure the fire's going properly in the drawing room. Central heating is one thing, but you need to see some flames to feel properly warm when it's snowing.'

Maggie was pulling gently at Emma's arm. 'Come upstairs,' she invited. 'You'll love this room. So much better than a hotel, I promise.'

Perhaps it was best if she stayed for one night, Emma thought. It might only be mid-afternoon but it was already looking a lot darker outside and what if she went hunting for a hotel room and couldn't find one? She would hardly want to start her first shift in an unfamiliar emergency department having slept in her vehicle overnight. Besides, she had to admit she was curious. She wanted to see more of this impressive house. She also couldn't deny that part of her wanted to know what was going on in Max Cunningham's life. It almost felt like they had something in common here, in that their lives weren't turning out how they might have anticipated—or wanted—when they'd last been in each other's company.

The sweep of the wide staircase was dramatic enough to conjure up images of women making a grand entrance in exquisite ball gowns. The first part of the hallway it led to looked down over the entrance foyer. Emma could see Dr Cunningham senior disappearing through a door with his dog by his heels. She could also see Max, who was simply standing still as if he was taking a breath in order to size up an accident scene, perhaps. Or what looked like it might be a complicated resuscitation.

The way he cradled his forehead in his hand a heartbeat later, rubbing both his temples with his thumb and middle finger, added to the impression of a man out of his depth, and it was enough to touch Emma's heart. She knew, better than most, how life had a habit of side-swiping you sometimes and it never hurt to offer kindness.

Sometimes, it could save a life.

'Here you are.' Maggie stopped at one of several doors further down the hallway. 'This one's got its own bathroom so it will be perfect for you, I think.'

Emma followed her into the room. She could actually feel her jaw dropping. A four-poster bed? A massive wardrobe and dressing table that looked like museum pieces, an ornate fireplace with leather armchairs positioned in front of it and a cushioned window seat set into the mullioned window. The floorboards were polished wood but there was a large rug with a Persian design.

'I hope it doesn't smell musty,' Maggie said. 'I've only had a day or two to change linen and try and air things out. Some of these rooms haven't been used since Max and Andy left home and that's a very long time ago, now.'

'Who's Andy?' Emma was still gazing around the room. Her earliest years had been in a small Italian village. Her recent years had been in a cramped one-bedroom flat in central London. She'd only ever been in houses like this when she'd paid an entry fee and stood behind the braided red ropes.

'Max's younger brother.' Maggie had been leading the way to an interior door that must lead to the en-suite bathroom but now she paused. 'He hasn't told you what's going on, has he?'

Curiosity battled with an odd sense of... what was it? A desire to protect Max—or at least his privacy—perhaps?

'It's probably none of my business,' she said quickly.

'Nonsense.' Maggie flapped her hand. 'You're part of it for the time being, anyway, so you may as well know. The children that are arriving here any minute are Andy's children. They're orphans now and Max is their legal guardian.'

Wow... No wonder Max was looking like he was about to face a daunting situation. Everybody had known that he was a diehard bachelor even a decade ago. And while he'd been great with the children on that paediatric ward, he'd confessed more than once that that was because he could hand them back to their parents. Or get a nurse to change a nappy or deal with any tears and tantrums. That he'd never want to have any of his own.

And he'd just lost his brother?

'I'm so sorry,' Emma said. 'I really shouldn't be intruding. Not when the Cunninghams have just lost such a close family member.'

Maggie shook her head. 'Andy died just over a year ago. And his marriage had fallen apart a year or more before that. They did try and work things out, and that must have been when Alice was conceived, but then it turned nasty and lawyers got involved. Simone moved away, broke a court order and took the kids with her and broke Andy's heart at the same time. He died in a car accident not long after that. He'd been drinking and drove straight into a tree.'

'That's tragic...'

'Mmm.' Maggie hesitated for a moment and Emma wondered if there was more to that accident than simply drink-driving but if the housekeeper had been about to voice her own opinion, she obviously changed her mind. 'Even worse, Simone wouldn't let the family have anything more to do with the children after Andy was gone. She was living up in Scotland and Dr Cunningham didn't even hear about her death until after her funeral. Until someone in Social Services had tracked down legal documents that gave Max guardianship.' Maggie was moving again.

'Come and see your bathroom. There should be everything you might need.'

Emma took in the clawfoot iron bath with its brass tapware, separate shower and shelves piled with fluffy towels. 'It's beautiful.'

'It is.' Maggie smiled. 'This was the master suite in the early days when the boys were little ones. Dr Cunningham senior couldn't bear to stay in it after his wife died and then he decided he'd just stay in the Green Room. Oh…is that a car I can hear?' She walked swiftly to the window and peered down. 'It is. I'd better go and help. There was supposed to have been a nanny here already to be with the children but she got sick and that's why you're here. To cover Max at work so that he can stay home to look after them all.'

Unsure of what she should do, Emma followed the housekeeper. Her head was spinning slightly with the tales of tragedy this family had experienced. What had happened to Max's mother? she wondered. And how old had Max and his brother been when she died? She was also trying to do a bit of maths in her head. If Andy had died over a year ago and his ex-wife had already been pregnant, then this baby Alice had to be at least several months old now. Not a newborn.

She could cope with that. For one night, it shouldn't be any problem at all, even if this wasn't exactly the kind of clinical situation that was part of her protective walls. As for Max—she had no idea how he was about to cope. He had years and years ahead of him as a guardian. Remembering the way he'd been cradling his head in his hands when he thought he was not being observed, Emma couldn't believe that he'd magically changed his attitude to children in the last ten years and would be quite happy to be sharing his life with them from now on.

'Where are they?' Maggie opened the front door but there was no sign of a car. 'Oh, no… they must have gone through to the clinic parking.'

'There's another car.' Max was standing beside her.

James Cunningham had come into the entrance foyer to see what was going on but Emma hung back, near the staircase, wondering if she should, in fact, go back upstairs for a while. How terrifying would it be for small children to arrive and be faced with so many strangers? Even if they'd met these members of their extended family it had apparently been more than a year ago and they would still be traumatised by the loss of their mother.

Through the wide gap of the open front door, she could see a large people-carrier type van that had parked a little way away from the entrance to the house and someone was getting out of the driver's seat. Max walked out into the snow that was still falling to greet the newcomer. But someone else was running towards the front door of the house from the opposite direction. A middle-aged woman who was looking very anxious.

'Dr Cunningham? Is the clinic closed already?'

'Surgery finished an hour ago, Jenny.' But James was frowning. 'What's wrong?'

'It's Terry. He's got terrible chest pain and his spray isn't helping. He wouldn't let me call an ambulance. It was all I could do to persuade him to come and see you and he only did that because you're right next door.'

Behind Jenny, Emma could see that children were being helped out of the van. A boy who might be about six or seven. A smaller girl. The driver was opening the back hatch which looked to be full of luggage and items like a pram and cot. Max was unclipping a baby seat. Emma's mouth went a little dry. Maybe this was going to be harder to cope with than she'd thought.

James looked towards where his grandchildren were being ushered towards him. He turned his head to look in the other direction, presumably to the 'west wing' that housed his general practice clinic. His duty lay in both directions, with the professional one clearly more urgent than the personal.

And, suddenly, Emma knew exactly how she could help everyone here, including herself. Years of honing her skills to be able to work to the best of her ability in unfamiliar places made it automatic to take charge but, as a bonus, it felt as if her protective walls were suddenly strengthening themselves around her and keeping her in her safe space. She walked towards the anxious woman.

'I'm Dr Moretti,' she told her. 'I can help you.'

Only a couple of minutes later, Emma was opening the door to the clinic with one of the keys on the ring James had given her.

'There's a twelve-lead ECG machine in the treatment room,' he'd told her. 'If it looks like an infarct, call an ambulance and then let me know.'

'I can handle it,' Emma had promised.

Jenny and her husband, Terry, followed her into what was clearly a waiting room.

'How's the pain level, Terry? On a scale of zero to ten, with zero being no pain at all and ten being the worst you could imagine?'

'Seven,' Terry told her. 'It's like a knife in my chest. It's hard to breathe, even.'

'Let's get you lying down so I can have a good look at you.' Emma walked ahead, opening one door and then another. There was a small kitchen, a storeroom, a consulting room and…yes…what looked like a treatment room, well set up for minor procedures or more extensive assessments. She recognised the machine for taking a twelve-lead ECG, spotted an oxygen cylinder in the corner of the room and was relieved to see a defibrillator on another trolley. If Terry was having a heart attack and in any danger of an imminent cardiac arrest she had the means to deal with it. She also knew that one of the keys on the ring she was holding was to open a drug cabinet that James had told her was well stocked.

On first impressions, Terry didn't look like a man who was in the middle of having a heart attack. His colour was good, he wasn't sweating and he seemed to be clutching the side of his chest rather than a more classic sign of pressing his hand to the centre. He'd also told her that he wasn't feeling sick in any way but Emma wasn't about to make assumptions. She helped her patient climb onto the bed and lifted the back so he wasn't lying completely flat.

'Let's get that coat and jumper off and unbutton your shirt, Terry.' Emma opened the

drawer on the ECG trolley and took out electrodes. 'So you've been getting angina for a
while?'

'Just a bit. And only when I'm doing too
much.'

'He's taken up jogging,' his wife told
Emma. 'I told him he's going to kill himself
but he's determined to lose the weight.'

'And you were jogging when the chest pain
came on?'

'No...' Terry lifted his arm out of the way
as Emma stuck the final electrodes on the left
side of his chest. 'I was getting the damned
turkey out of the freezer in the barn.'

'It was far too big to go in the freezer in
the house.' Jenny nodded. 'And it takes days
and days to thaw.'

'It was like carrying a giant, slippery rock,'
Terry complained. 'And then I started to drop
it and almost tripped over something at the
same time and it went flying.' He gave a huff
of something like laughter that turned into a
groan. 'So to speak... Anyway, it was when
I bent down and picked the turkey up that the

pain came on. By the time I got it into the laundry tub, I could hardly stand up.'

'Does anything make it worse?' Emma asked, still smiling at Terry's attempt at humour. 'Like taking a deep breath?'

Terry tried to breathe in and groaned. 'Yep...that really hurts.'

'And you used your angina spray?'

'Didn't do a thing.'

'Okay.' Emma was becoming more confident that she wasn't dealing with a critical cardiac event. 'Keep really still for me for a few seconds, Terry. I'm going to do the ECG.'

With the sheet of graph paper in her hand a short time later, Emma smiled at the anxious couple in front of her.

'Good news,' she told them. 'This all looks absolutely normal. There's no sign of your pain being due to angina and certainly no indication that you're having a heart attack.'

'Oh...' Jenny started to cry. 'I was *so* worried.'

'What is it, then?' Terry asked.

Emma handed Jenny the box of tissues. 'I suspect you pulled a muscle between your ribs while you were wrestling with that frozen turkey,' she told him. She put her hand on the left side of his chest. 'Tell me if this hurts...'

Jenny stayed by the head of the bed, watched the thorough examination her husband was receiving and listened to the advice about cold and heat packs and using anti-inflammatory medication.

'Are you sure it's not a heart attack?' she asked.

'Quite sure.' Emma smiled. 'But you did the right thing in getting it checked out. I'm going to take your blood pressure while you're here too, Terry.'

'Imagine if it *had* been a heart attack.' Jenny reached for another tissue. 'Right before Christmas. I know it's terrible at any time of year but there's something about Christmas, isn't there?'

'Mmm...' Emma stuck the earpieces of a stethoscope into place as a hint for Jenny to stop talking. She didn't need a reminder of how much worse it was to have a tragedy at Christmas time. She placed the disc of the stethoscope over the artery in Terry's elbow as she pumped up the blood pressure cuff.

Jenny hadn't taken the hint. 'It's like the poor Cunninghams. Ruined Christmas forever for those poor boys. They used to call it "the Cunninghams' Christmas Curse" in these parts.'

Emma knew she shouldn't encourage gossip but it wasn't as if she'd asked a question aloud. Her startled glance had been enough to prompt Jenny to continue.

'Their poor mother,' she said sadly. 'Fought off the cancer for such a long time and all she wanted was one last Christmas with her little boys but they didn't even get the decorations up.' She lowered her voice. 'And they've never been put up again, from what I heard. Not in that house...'

Emma let the pressure out of the cuff slowly. Concentrating on the figures as she heard a pulse begin and then disappear again didn't stop part of her brain absorbing the information she'd just been given. What a sad house this must have been for Max—especially that first Christmas without his mother.

'Your blood pressure is on the high end of normal,' she told Terry. 'Are you on any medication for that?'

'Yes. Dr Cunningham looks after me well, don't you worry about that. Can I get dressed again now?'

'And then there was last year.' Jenny handed her husband his jumper as he finished buttoning up his shirt. 'Losing poor Andy like that. It shouldn't have happened at all, but to have it happen in December. Another Christmas funeral...' She clicked her tongue. 'And now...those children... What sort of Christmas is this going to be for those poor wee mites?'

Terry's head popped out of the jumper's neck. 'That's enough, Jen,' he said quietly. 'I'm sure Dr Moretti isn't interested in hearing all this gossip.'

'It's not gossip,' Jenny said defensively. 'We care about each other in Upper Barnsley, that's all. Especially our closest neighbours.' She smiled at Emma. 'Are you here to help Dr Cunningham, then? It's about time he had another doctor to help him in this clinic.

Young Max is brilliant but he's always been one for an exciting life. He doesn't want to leave that big emergency department at the hospital.'

'I'm actually here to help at the hospital,' Emma told them. 'But, right now, I'm going to go and show Dr Cunningham your ECG, Terry, and let him know that you're okay.' She held the door open for the couple. 'Have you got plenty of anti-inflammatories at home?'

'Oh, yes.' Jenny nodded. 'And don't go bothering Dr Cunningham with my Terry's problems right now. I suspect he's got enough of his own...'

'You need to follow the directions on the tin for how many scoops. Level scoops, like this...' Maggie scooped the formula and showed Max how to level it off with the back of a knife. 'Put it into the bottle of warm water. Attach the nipple and ring and cap like this...and then shake it.'

Maybe baby Alice could smell the milk being prepared and she was sick of waiting. Or maybe she didn't like the unfamiliar male arms that were holding her right now. What-ever the reason, her unhappy whimpers were steadily increasing into shrieks that were pulling the tense knots in Max's gut tighter by the second.

'Are you sure you can't stay, Maggie?'

'I'm sorry, Max, but it's impossible. I've got my daughter, Ruth, arriving and she's nearly eight months pregnant and on her own. She'll be exhausted after that long drive up from Cornwall and I haven't had proper time with her since that bastard of a boyfriend walked out on her a few weeks ago. We've got a lot of talking to do about how she's going to cope.' Maggie took the cap off the bottle and up-ended it. 'Shake a few drops onto your wrist, like this. If it's the right temperature it won't feel either hot or cold. There…that's per-fect.' She held the bottle out to Max. 'Try that. She's probably eating solids now as well and there's plenty of baby food in with all that other shopping that's in the pantry but she'll be wanting her milk for comfort right now, I expect.'

He took the bottle and offered the teat to the

baby. Alice turned her head away and arched into his arm as if she was trying to escape.

'Take her into the drawing room with the others,' Maggie suggested. 'This is all new and strange for her too, and it might help if you're sitting in a comfy chair with her brother and sister nearby.'

Max walked out of the kitchen and into an entranceway that looked like it had exploded into a collection point for a children's charity over the last thirty minutes or so. A portable cot had a few stuffed toys and books in it. There were car seats and a pram and even a high chair, along with boxes of baby supplies like nappies and formula and suitcases that he'd been told were full of clothing. The social worker who had delivered the children and their belongings had been apologetic but in a hurry to get away before the snow started settling on the country roads and Maggie, who'd done far more than anything her part-time position with the Cunninghams had ever expected of her, was obviously worried about leaving the men to cope but also anxious to get back to her own family.

'You go, Maggie,' Max told her. 'I've got this.'

The older woman gave him a searching look. 'Are you sure?' she asked quietly. 'I don't want to leave you in the lurch. Ruth would understand if...'

Max shook his head. 'These children are my responsibility,' he said. 'Between us, Dad and I will figure it out.' He joggled the baby in his arms and, for a merciful few seconds, the howling seemed to lessen.

'You've got that lovely Emma to help, for tonight at least.' Maggie was heading for the coat rack. 'If you're sure, then... I'll come back as soon as I can in the morning if the roads are clear enough.'

As she opened the door, Max could see a car disappearing down the driveway. Emma had spent a good deal of time assessing that unexpected patient who had turned up but she hadn't summoned an ambulance or come to find his father so he had assumed things were under control. Some things, anyway. Baby Alice was crying again as he went into the drawing room.

His father was sitting in his usual chair by the fire but Pirate had disappeared beneath the chair, which was highly unusual. On the sofa next to the chair were the two older children, Ben and Matilda. They were both sitting silently, side by side, holding hands. Six-year-old Ben was clutching a very small artificial Christmas tree in his other hand that was devoid of any decorations. Four-year-old Matilda had a toy rabbit with long legs and rather chewed-looking ears clamped under her arm. They both looked accusingly at their uncle when he came in carrying their miserable baby sister.

Max sat in the matching leather wing chair on the other side of the sofa, settled Alice into the crook of his elbow and tried to get her to accept her bottle again. Her renewed cries were so loud he didn't hear the door opening. He didn't notice that every other head in the room had turned to see who was coming in or that Pirate had wriggled forward enough to peer out from under the chair.

What he did become aware of was that fresh lemony scent he'd noticed when Emma had come into his office in what was beginning to feel like a previous lifetime. And when he looked up, it felt like the depth of understanding in Emma's eyes told him that she knew exactly how far out of his depth he currently was. That, no matter how determined he was to do the right thing for his nieces and nephew, it felt like he was drowning. But there was something else in her eyes that looked as though she was tapping into something much deeper. Darker.

Fear...

But why would Emma Moretti, of all people, feel afraid when faced with a miserable, hungry infant? She'd been the first to offer cuddles or bottles to their small patients in that paediatric ward, the first in line to be present at a birth or do the newborn checks on those slippery, squiggly little bundles that Max had found quite alarming at the time. If anything, he would have expected her to scoop Alice out of his arms and rescue the situation like some sort of Christmas angel, albeit with dark eyes and hair and olive skin instead of peaches and cream and blue eyes and golden hair.

But she was just staring at him and…yes… he was sure he could see fear in those astonishingly dark eyes.

What on earth had happened, he wondered, to have changed her like this?

The curiosity was fleeting, however, because despite Alice's cries still increasing in volume, he could hear the landline of the house ringing from the hallway. His father seemed oblivious, slumped in his chair as if he had no idea quite how to deal with what was going on around him. Emma had clearly heard the sound of the telephone and the way she raised her eyebrows was an offer to go and answer the call but Max acted without really thinking. He could handle a phone call far better than what he was trying to cope with right now.

He walked towards Emma and shoved Alice at her, knowing that she would instinctively hold out her arms to take the baby. Then he passed her the bottle of milk, turned away and walked out of the room.

CHAPTER THREE

EMMA WATCHED IN horror as Max walked out
of the room and left her—literally—holding
the baby.

And maybe Alice was significantly older
and heavier than a newborn but, for a heartbeat, Emma simply froze because this baby
wasn't sick and she wasn't standing here in
the capacity of a doctor. This baby needed
feeding and she had just been forced into the
position of being a surrogate mother—something she wouldn't have volunteered for in a
million years.

Turning away from watching Max leave,
Emma found herself looking at the two small
children who were sitting on the couch and
staring at her. They both looked scared. That
something terrible was happening with their
baby sister, perhaps?

'It's okay,' Emma heard herself saying calmly. 'I think she's just hungry.'

She could do something about that, she realised, and that was the only thing she needed to think about right now. Anything else, including how this was making her feel, would simply have to wait but, as she moved to sit down, it seemed that the shock of having the baby shoved into her arms was receding enough to make it bearable. She would certainly not have volunteered to take the baby and feed it but, now that it was happening, Emma found that it hadn't smashed through her walls the way she might have feared that it would. This was someone else's baby, not her own. A healthy baby that just needed to be fed. Surely she could cope with this?

She chose to sit on the couch beside the other children, not wanting to take over the chair Max had been using. Or maybe she thought it might comfort the infant in her arms to be near her brother and sister. She settled Alice into the crook of her arm and offered her the nipple of the bottle, sliding it into her mouth that was opening for a new wail. Surprised eyes stared up at her and then, mercifully, that little mouth closed over the teat and Alice began sucking vigorously.

In the sudden silence that fell, Emma was aware that the older children were still watching. Max's father had turned to peer at her from behind the wing of his chair and even the dog had wriggled forwards far enough to see what was happening beyond the safety of being beneath his master's chair. She could hear the fire behind its screen, crackling softly in this new silence, and then she could hear Max coming back into the room. Or maybe she could feel the change in the atmosphere as he entered—that kind of electricity that charismatic people radiated.

'That was the builder,' he said. 'They've fixed the leak in the apartment above mine but it's going to be a big job to get things fixed and cleaned up. It certainly won't be happening before Christmas.'

James Cunningham grunted. 'Can't say I'm surprised. It's hard enough to get tradesmen in a hurry at the best of times.'

Max sat down in the other wing chair, his

gaze fixed on Alice. 'You always did make it look easy,' he murmured. 'You're just a natural, aren't you, Emma?'

Emma said nothing. She couldn't say anything. Not with that damned lump that had just formed in her throat. Breathe, she told herself. You only need to breathe.

The silence returned and then Max sounded like he was making an effort to break it.

'Is that your special Christmas tree, Ben?'

Emma glanced sideways to see Ben nod solemnly. 'You've got to have a Christmas tree,' he told his uncle. 'It's a rule.'

'Oh?'

Emma could understand the note in Max's voice—as if he was wondering what other 'rules' Ben might be holding as sacrosanct.

Ben nodded again. 'That's how Father Christmas knows where to leave the presents. It should go near the chimney.'

Emma lifted her gaze to look around the huge room they were in. She wondered what this little boy might think of those paintings in their ornate frames, the ornaments on sideboards and the baby grand piano in the corner. Was he used to this kind of house or was it making this an even more frightening experience for him?

But Ben was sounding worried rather than frightened when he spoke again.

'Where's *your* Christmas tree, Grandpa?'

This time, the silence in the room was filled with a tension that made a knot start to form in Emma's stomach. There was level upon level of misery here that she could feel as if it was her own. Some of it *was* her own but she had learned long ago how to shut that away and it was actually quite empowering to find she could hold and feed baby Alice without falling apart in any visible manner. Looking down, she met the fixed gaze of those dark baby eyes on her own and could be confident that all was well in this tiny human's life for the moment, at least, as she sucked down the rest of her milk. It wasn't the case for anyone else in this room, was it?

Emma looked at the children beside her on the couch. The little boy was still staring at his grandfather, waiting for an answer to his question about the missing Christmas tree. The little girl seemed to sense Emma's gaze and returned it with such a solemn one of her own that, if her arms weren't full of baby Alice and her bottle, she would have instinctively wanted to gather this child to her as closely as she could to give her a big hug. James was stroking an imaginary beard as if it might help him find an answer and Max...

Well, Max was looking at *her.*

As if he knew that she knew why Christmas hadn't been celebrated in this house for probably decades and why a simple child's question was creating such tension. As if he had no idea how to defuse it and as if he was trusting her to help in the same way that she had managed to conquer the difficulty he had faced in getting the baby fed.

Just for a heartbeat, Emma could see something she was quite sure she'd never seen before in Max Cunningham's eyes. Bewilderment, almost. The look of someone who'd lost something very important and had absolutely no idea where to start looking for it. There was something sad in that gaze as well and that made her realise he must know exactly how his nephew must be feeling right now and that could be what was making it so hard for him to find the right thing to say. A tragic history had repeated itself and a small boy had lost his mum just before Christmas.

The squeeze on Emma's heart was so tight it was painful. Painful enough to set off alarm bells that suggested a potential breach in any protective walls that needed maintaining but she had to ignore that for the moment. She was an adult and she had had plenty of time to develop coping mechanisms she could tap into a bit later. Doing something to try and make these children look and sound a little less sad was far more urgent.

'Sometimes,' she told Ben, quietly, 'things happen that can get in the way of remembering rules. I'm sure your Uncle Max or your Grandpa will know where to find a Christmas tree.'

James leaned forward to pick up a poker and prod the fire, making a grumbling sound that could have been disapproving but Max was nodding as if this was, indeed, the solution.

'A real one,' he said. 'We can go and look in the woods tomorrow, Ben. You can choose a branch and I'll cut it off. Or, if we can't find one, we can drive into town and buy one.'

'How old are you, Ben?' Emma asked.

'Six.'

'That's old enough to make decorations for the tree, then. Like silver stars. I can show you how to do that.' She offered a smile. 'My name's Emma.'

The little girl was wriggling closer. 'I'm four,' she whispered, 'and I like stars...'

'You can help too, sweetheart,' Emma promised. She just had to hope there would be a supply of cardboard and silver foil somewhere in the house.

'That's Matilda,' Max said. 'But she likes to be called Tilly.' He was smiling at Emma.

And it was such a genuine smile... Nothing like the charm-loaded curl of his lips with that mischievous edge that had always won him so much attention from women. This time, that automatic hint of flirting that Emma had remembered so clearly was completely absent and it changed his face. It made him look a little older. Softer—as if he was perfectly capable of providing the care and commitment these children were going to need so badly even if he used to say it was the last thing he ever wanted to do.

Alice had finished her bottle and felt sleepy and relaxed. Emma shifted her to an upright position and began to rub her back. Seconds later, the loud burp broke both the new silence and quite a lot of the tension in the room.

'I'm hungry,' Ben said.

Emma caught the slightly panicked glance that was exchanged between the two Cunningham men.

'Maggie's left a pie in the oven,' Max told his father. 'And chips.'

'I like chips.' Ben slid off the couch. He stood there, waiting for one of the grown-ups to move as well.

But, for a long moment, nobody did and Emma could understand why. This was it, wasn't it? The first step into a life that was never going to be the same again for either of these men and it was huge and daunting and they'd been thrown into the deep end. None of it was Emma's responsibility, of course, but the people who were going to suffer if it turned into a disaster were only children and these children had suffered enough, hadn't they?

It seemed that Max was thinking the same thing because they both got to their feet in the same moment. He stepped towards Emma and took the sleeping baby from her arms.

'It's okay,' he said. 'I can manage.'

'I'm here,' Emma reminded him gently. 'I may as well help you manage for tonight, yes?'

There was always something about a man holding a baby that tugged at the heartstrings. But there was something else about this particular man holding a baby that actually brought a lump to Emma's throat. This had to be his worst nightmare, inheriting a ready-made family including a baby, but he was stepping up to the challenge and determined to do his best and that was courageous and kind and…it tugged at her heart so hard she couldn't look away from his eyes.

She hadn't remembered them being quite such a dark blue.

Or quite so…intense.

It almost felt as if he was seeing her…*really* seeing her…for the first time ever.

Man…

Those eyes… So dark they looked bottomless. You could fall into eyes like that and get totally lost. And, just for a heartbeat, that was exactly what Max wanted to do. The rollercoaster of emotions he was currently riding was proving even more overwhelming than he'd feared it would be.

His heart had gone out to his nephew and nieces the moment he'd seen them but he was little more than a stranger to them and, oddly, that hurt. There was so much stuff that had come with the children and he wouldn't have even known how to make up a bottle if Maggie hadn't helped. He might have failed in feeding Alice if he hadn't forced Emma to help so he could add a sense of failure into the mix. He was worried about how his father was coping, especially after that question about the Christmas tree. They hadn't put a tree up in this house since his mother had died, leaving a huge pine tree undecorated and a shattered family that barely noticed the showers of dead needles that came weeks later.

On top of that, there were feelings of heartbreak for these children. Part of him just wanted to gather them all into his arms and somehow let them know that he was going to protect them for ever, but he could sense their shyness and knew he would make things worse if he tried to force closeness. He felt gratitude to Maggie for all her extra work and, currently, he was just so, so glad that Emma was here in the house. Trying to convince her that he was up to this task was giving him a lot more courage than he might have otherwise found in the face of such a daunting challenge.

There was also the way she'd been looking at him after Ben had asked about where the Christmas tree was. It had made him think that she knew the answer to that innocent question, which was not unlikely given that she'd spent time with Terry and Jenny. Jenny wasn't a gossip by any means but she was one of the villagers who all knew the Cunninghams' history and she was a woman who loved to chat. Max didn't mind if Emma did know because there was also something in that look that gave him the impression that she understood how much it might hurt and, in turn, that was giving him the oddest feeling of connection. Something that was disconcerting because he'd never associated a feeling like that with any woman. It had to be just another side effect of this strange situation. It was also something that was irrelevant because the children were the only people that mattered right now.

'What's first?' he asked. 'Shall I feed the children?'

'How 'bout you and your dad sort some of their things out? Find things like pyjamas and toothbrushes? You could put Alice in her pram for the moment while she's asleep. Show me where the kitchen is and I'll sort out the pie.'

'And chips.' The small voice came from

right beside Max's leg and he looked down to find Ben standing close by. 'And sauce. Red sauce.'

'Is that a rule?' Max asked. 'Red sauce for chips?'

Ben nodded. He was holding out his hand towards Matilda. 'Come on, Tilly,' he said. 'It's time for tea.'

'It is,' Emma said, as Matilda slid off the couch. 'And after that it will be bath time and…what happens after bath time?'

'Storytime,' Ben said. 'And…and then…'

His small mouth wobbled as it turned down at the corners. It was painfully obvious that the prospect of bedtime in this new, scary house was too much even for a very brave child who was doing his best to look after his younger sister himself. The squeeze in Max's chest was so sharp it made the back of his eyes prickle. He bent down so that he could say something quietly, just for Ben.

'It's going to be okay,' he whispered. 'I promise.'

Ben's eyes were a dark blue. Like his father's had been. Like all the Cunningham men, for that matter. They were also far too serious for a six-year-old boy.

'It's a new rule,' Max added gravely. 'And I try very hard to never break rules.'

Having so much to do to start getting the children settled into what was going to be their new home was helpful for the next few hours. Having Emma there to answer the questions James and Max kept coming up with was also very helpful.

'Should we put Alice's cot in the same room as Tilly and Ben?'

'It might be better to put it in your room to start with. That way, if she wakes up, she won't wake up the others.'

'But…what will I do with her if she does wake up?'

Emma's smile was kind enough not to make Max feel inadequate in any way. 'Give her a bottle of milk. Change her nappy. Cuddle her.'

Ben and Matilda ate enough of their dinner for Emma to be looking pleased when Max went to tell her that he had unpacked the suit-cases to find pyjamas.

'Shall we go up those big stairs?' She made it sound like an adventure. 'I know where there's a bath that's got feet.'

Ben shook his head. 'A bath doesn't have feet,' he told Emma. 'It can't walk.'

'No. This one just stands there but it really does have feet. Like a lion's paws. Do you want to see?'

Max watched her go up the stairs with a child on each side of her, holding her hands. Ben still had the little Christmas tree in his other hand, he noticed. And Tilly was hold-ing her rabbit by one foot so that its head, with those chewed ears, was bumping on every tread. James was coming down as they reached the halfway curve.

'Have you got hot-water bottles?' Emma asked him. 'It would be good to put them in Ben's and Tilly's beds. And put some of their toys there too, so it'll feel more like home.'

The men didn't get the distribution of stuffed toys quite right but it was easy enough to fix as the children climbed into the twin beds that were side by side in one of the smallest bedrooms. It was James who agreed to read a bedtime story to his grandchildren while Pirate lay outside the bedroom door. Max was learning how to bath Alice and get her ready for bed. At six months old she was nothing like as fragile as a newborn, of course, but she still felt very small in Max's hands and it was fiddly enough to get her into her nappy and her stretchy sleepsuit to make him break out in a bit of a sweat.

'So you've put her cot in your room?' Emma asked.

'Well…the room I use when I'm staying, yes. It might be a good one for the nanny to use when she gets here.'

'Have you plugged in the baby monitor?'

'Yes. And, if I leave the door open, I should be able to hear if Ben or Tilly wakes up too. You don't think they'll sleepwalk or anything, do you? What would I do if they did?'

'If they do get up, they'll just be looking for comfort,' Emma told him. 'Cuddles. You could stay with them until they go back to sleep. Or let them share your bed.'

There was a hint of mischief in Emma's eyes as she made that suggestion. As if she knew perfectly well that sharing a bed in order to comfort small children was a totally alien concept for Max. As if she was trying to lighten the atmosphere a little too, to defuse some of the tension of the evening. The idea that Emma might be at all concerned for his own wellbeing did make him feel rather a lot better, in fact.

'Are you hungry?' she asked. 'There's plenty of pie and chips left.'

'And red sauce?'

The smile he received from Emma felt like a reward for what seemed like a major achievement in caring for the children for the first time. Glancing at his watch, Max was astonished at how much time had gone by. 'It's late,' he said. 'No wonder I'm starving.'

'Let's see if we can get Alice settled properly. Your dad should be back from taking Pirate for a walk by then and we can all have something to eat.'

James came back with the news that, while the snow had settled in places, it seemed to have stopped and the roads were still clear enough to be safe for Emma to drive back into Cheltenham in the morning.

'And they're very good about getting the snow ploughs out on our road first,' he told her as they ate dinner together at the old table in the huge kitchen. 'One of the perks of being the only local doctor.'

'Do you do nights as well?' Emma asked.

It was Max who shook his head. 'Theoretically, that's covered by an afterhours service from town,' he told her. 'In reality, though, Dad often gets called.'

'I don't mind,' James said. 'I've known these families for a long time. They trust me. Thanks for taking care of Terry today, Emma. Jenny's still overanxious about his angina.'

'It was a pleasure.' Emma sounded as though she meant it.

James stood up to take his plate to the sink. 'Might turn in,' he said. 'It's been a big day.' He snapped his fingers and Pirate jumped out of his basket near the Aga. 'Can you look after the fire, Max?'

'Of course. Sleep well, Dad.'

The huff of sound was doubtful and the words were an under-the-breath mutter as James left the room. 'Let's hope we all get some sleep.'

Emma stacked the dishes into the dishwasher but Max wouldn't let her do anything else in the kitchen.

'Maggie will be back in the morning. Being used as a housekeeper or a nanny is not part of your locum contract, you know.'

Emma shrugged. 'They say that variety is the spice of life. To tell you the truth, I've never been in a house like this before and it's amazing.' Which it was. Every room she had seen in this old house was beautiful but her favourite so far had to be the kitchen, with its old range and the dresser with the antique china and an ancient scrubbed table that reminded her of outside terraces in Italy because it made her think of generations of extended family gathering to eat together. The time had flown, as well. They'd been so busy with dinner and baths and getting everybody settled into bed that Emma hadn't had time to worry about how it could potentially be messing with her head and, in fact, now that she did have the time to think about it, she was confident that she could deal with it.

'The children really haven't been much trouble, have they?' she said aloud. 'And the way Ben tries so hard to help look after Tilly is just gorgeous.'

'Mmm…'

The tone in that sound gave Emma's heart a squeeze as she pushed the door of the dishwasher closed. It was a note of trepidation. Fear, almost.

She caught his gaze. 'It's going to be okay, Max,' she said softly. 'You'll work things out. I know it feels huge and scary at the moment but just take it a day at a time. An hour at a time, if you need to.'

'Is that your strategy for when you find yourself in totally unfamiliar surroundings in your locum work?'

Emma smiled. 'Sometimes I'm taking it a second at a time. Oh…did you want some dessert? Ice cream, like the kids had, maybe?'

Max made another huff of sound. 'I think I need something a bit stronger than ice cream. Do you fancy a small whisky?'

Emma wrinkled her nose. 'I don't do whisky. A glass of wine would be nice, though. White, if you have any.'

'There's usually something in the fridge. Or there's rather a large wine cellar downstairs and it's cold enough at this time of year to be perfectly drinkable.'

The thought of being in a house that had a large wine cellar was as surreal as every other surprise this day had thrown at her. 'Just a small glass,' she warned. 'I've got a very early start tomorrow. I'll need to leave at least an hour to get into Cheltenham in case there's more snow in the night. More, if I need to put the chains on my tyres. And my shift starts at seven a.m., yes?'

'You're onto it.' Max was heading towards a large fridge. 'You sound like you could cope with anything, in fact.'

'It's part of what I like about locum work. You never quite know what's round the next corner. I've been out to remote islands off

Scotland in a boat. I did a stint with an air rescue service in Canada once too, and our agency specialises in insurance company work when an injured or ill traveller needs to get brought back home. I went out to an oil rig in a helicopter once.'

'Sounds exciting.'

'I love it. But it can be daunting as well. That's how I know that sometimes you need to focus on just the next step in front of you and block out the big picture.'

'I think I'd rather be on the way out to an oil rig than wondering what I'm going to do with unhappy children in the middle of the night.'

Emma took the glass of wine Max had poured for her. Her smile was one of both appreciation and, hopefully, some reassurance. The softening of his features and that hint of a smile told her that it seemed to have helped.

'Come in by the fire for a minute. I need to make that safe for the night and the whisky's in there too.'

And maybe he needed a bit more reassurance? Emma could provide that. For the sake of Max and his father. And those beautiful children. She'd been perfectly genuine when she'd told Max that the children hadn't been any trouble to look after and she was quite hopeful that she wasn't going to be kept awake tonight by ghosts from the past. Even when she had been helping Max bathe and dress the baby she had been able to keep that door in her own heart firmly closed. These children were like patients. Helping them was just an unexpected—and temporary—twist in her professional life.

It was no great hardship to take a few minutes to sit and sip an excellent wine in front of the fireplace, either. Despite the size of this impressive room, the flames created a flickering light and warmth that made the area directly in front of it seem homely. Almost intimate.

'So how long have you been working as a locum?' Max asked when they had chosen to sit at either end of the big couch rather than use the wing chairs.

'A bit over four years, now.' She had been offered bereavement leave but Emma had found she needed to get back to the job she loved so much, even though she'd been conscious of how hard it was going to be to work amongst young children and babies for a while. She'd learned to cope faster than she'd expected, however. She'd built those walls and kept going but some of the joy had gone and, as the months wore on, she'd known that if she wanted to move forward with her life and reclaim that joy, she needed to make some big changes. Hearing about someone's exciting career as a locum had happened at just the right time.

'If I'd ever thought about it, I would have said you'd be a consultant paediatrician by now.'

Emma tilted her head but didn't say anything. She could have agreed with him and said that was exactly what she'd been planning on being but, if she told him that, she'd have to tell him why it hadn't happened and she didn't want to go there. It was easier to focus on what else he'd just said that implied he'd never given her another thought after the time they'd worked together.

It was inevitable that that took her mind back to their kiss. The one *she'd* never forgotten...

Max broke the silence. 'I guess none of us know what twists and turns life has in store for us. We just know that they're going to happen—usually at what seems to be the worst possible time.'

'Mmm.' Emma could certainly agree with that. For a long moment, they both sipped their drinks and the silence was companionable. She knew she might be taking a risk that could destroy this pleasant ambience but Emma was curious. There was so much about Max that she'd never known. Would never have guessed.

'How old were you when your mum died, Max?' she asked gently.

His glance was swift. Intense. 'So Jenny did tell you? Or was it Maggie?'

'They both told me a little. Not much. Maggie told me about your brother. Jenny said something about your mother.'

'Something about the "Curse of the Cunninghams", perhaps?'

Embarrassed, Emma dropped her gaze. She'd hate Max to think she'd been gossiping about his family.

'It's okay,' he said with a sigh. 'I know people like to talk and it's no wonder it's all resurfacing now. Here it is, Christmas again, and tragedy number three strikes the Cunningham family.'

'That should be it, then.'

'Sorry?'

'Bad things are supposed to come in threes.' Emma bit her lip. The tragedies that had befallen this family were nothing to make light of but all she wanted to do was offer…something. Comfort wasn't possible but perhaps some hope? 'Christmas will be different this year.' She offered a smile this time. 'I'm sure the tree will just be the first of all the rules that Ben knows about.'

Max snorted. 'Christmas rules are just part of the commercial hype that's all this season is all about. Reasons to make you spend more and more money.'

'You think?'

'I don't imagine this is the first Christmas

you've worked so you know about the effects of the kind of stress it creates. People drink too much. Domestic violence goes through the roof. It's marketed as a promise for peace and love for everyone who bothers to follow all those "rules" but anyone who stands back far enough can see it for what it is.'

There was a defensiveness in his tone that made Emma think he was protesting too much. Because he'd had to—to protect himself? Because it was so much harder if you let yourself sink into what was missing from a celebration of family? She, of all people, could understand that.

'I don't believe that,' she said quietly. 'I'm not saying it's not a particularly difficult time for a lot of people but, if you're lucky, it's an opportunity to hit pause for a day. To celebrate the things that are really important—like family and friends. And, yes, we do that by buying stuff and eating special food but that's okay too, because it's all part of what makes it special. And they're not "rules". They're traditions and every family makes their own. I expect Ben is holding onto the ones he knows about as tightly as he can because he's lost just about everything else.'

Emma had to stop talking then, so that she could swallow the lump in her throat. She could feel Max's gaze resting on her.

'So…why aren't you with *your* family, then? You do have one, don't you?'

Emma nodded. 'In Italy. We have quite different traditions there. Like the feast of the seven fishes on Christmas Eve—the *Festa dei Sette Pesci*. And there's always a nativity scene in the house and someone gets chosen to put the baby Jesus in the crib on Christmas Eve.' She let her breath out in a sigh. 'I haven't been back home for a few years, though.'

'Why not?'

'As a locum, it can be one of the busiest times of the year because so many people want time off to be with their families.' Emma closed her eyes for a heartbeat, ignoring the faint alarm bell in her head. She had, albeit unintentionally, stepped into a private part of Max Cunningham's life. It was only fair if he knew a little more about her, wasn't it? 'Plus, I had a pretty rough Christmas a few years back and I needed some time out. Especially from my family, who would have insisted on talking about it endlessly.'

'What happened?'

'Um…well, it started a bit before Christmas, I guess, when the guy I thought I was going to marry walked out on me. But then… someone special died…'

'At Christmas time?'

'On Christmas Day.' Emma gulped in some air. 'I knew it was coming but that doesn't necessarily make it any easier at the time, you know?'

'Oh, yeah…' Max's tone was heartfelt. 'I know.' It was his turn to take a deeper breath. 'I didn't answer your question before. I was eleven when my mum died. My brother Andy was only eight. Not much older than Ben.'

'Oh, Max… I'm so sorry. That must have been so hard for you all.'

'I think we were too shocked to think about Christmas that year. It was the next one that was the hardest. Andy wanted it to be like it had been, but it was too hard on Dad. I found him crying and that shocked me so much. I had no idea what to do.'

'Of course you didn't. You were a child.'

'I'm not proud of what I did do.'

Emma watched the way Max's face creased into lines of regret. 'I'm sure it wasn't that bad.'

'I told Andy that Father Christmas wasn't real. That it had been Mum who'd put all the decorations up and all those presents under the tree and in our stockings and that, now she wasn't here, it couldn't happen any more because it would make Dad too sad.'

Oh… Emma could just imagine the serious conversation between two small boys. A fragmented family trying to find a way to be together without it causing too much pain for anyone. It was heartbreaking.

'So it didn't happen that year. Or the next. And then we just got used to it. We'd give each other a gift but we never put up a Christmas tree again or did any of the other decorations that Mum used to love—like winding long ropes of artificial leafy stuff like ivy and holly with its red berries between the bannisters on the staircase and hanging little bunches of golden bells on every door so that they jingled whenever they were opened and closed. Andy started doing it all again once he had children of his own, mind you.' Max drained his glass. 'Me, I just got more cynical about it all but then, it only really matters for the kids, doesn't it?'

'I'm not sure about that,' Emma said slowly. 'But it's certainly a very special time of the year for children. Exciting…and magical, until you know the truth about Father Christmas.'

Max grimaced. 'Don't worry. I'm not about to burst the bubble for Ben or Tilly. They've got more than enough of real life to get their heads around at the moment.'

'But…' Again, Emma bit her lip. This really wasn't any of her business.

'But, what?'

'It's just that…well…putting up a Christmas tree is only a part of it. And it's only a decoration if you don't really believe…'

'In Father Christmas?'

Emma shook her head. 'No. In family. In

celebrating the bond. Or, in your case this year, perhaps it's about creating a bond. The new one that's going to be the foundation for Ben and Tilly and Alice to feel like they belong.'

Max was staring at her. 'I can't do that.'

'You can. You and your dad. All you have to do is love these children and I'm sure you do already.'

'Yes, but...we don't know how to do Christmas. It's been more than twenty years since we even had a piece of tinsel in the house. Dad wouldn't want it.'

'Are you sure? It's been a long time, Max. Sometimes it takes a gentle push to get people past something that's holding them back. This new family of yours is a gift. It could turn out to be the best thing that could have happened.'

'The breaking of the curse?'

'If you like. The start of something new, anyway. Something very special.'

Emma's tone had softened as she thought about these two bachelor men of different generations sharing their lives with three small children. About the amount of love that would be available within the thick stone walls of this ancient house. She was smiling at Max as she finished speaking. He was holding her gaze with that kind of intensity she had felt before—when it had seemed like he was really seeing her for the first time.

'You're right,' he said softly. 'This could be the most important Christmas these kids will ever have. It *has* to be special.' He still hadn't broken the eye contact and Emma was starting to feel an odd tingle spreading through her body.

'You have to help me, Emma. Please...' The plea in Max's tone was so heartfelt. 'I don't know how to do this by myself. I... I need you...'

The tingle had just reached Emma's toes.

'We *all* need you,' Max added, as if summoning every power of persuasion he could find. 'Me and Dad. Ben and Tilly and Alice. Probably Pirate too. Just to be here when you're not at the hospital. Just to be...well... just to be *you*... And...and you did promise to show Ben and Tilly how to make stars and we didn't get time to do that tonight, did we?'

Emma nodded. 'I did say I'd show them how to make stars.'

But to stay here in this house?

To spend Christmas with a family?

It was terrifying and compelling at the same time. Emma knew she should run a mile but there was something in her way.

Maybe it was a small boy with solemn eyes. A little girl with a bunny that had chewed ears or a baby that had been watching her as if she was the most important person on earth as she'd sucked her bottle. Perhaps it was a man of her father's generation who loved his little dog but had lost the joy of this season so long ago. Or…maybe it was this man who was looking lost but was so determined to do his best for the entire little family that had just turned up on his doorstep. A man who wanted her to be here. Who *needed* her…

Christmas… With children. And a baby. How could she possibly cope with saying yes?

But Max needed her. Perhaps everybody

needed her because she was outside the tragedy that had brought them together so maybe
she could see what needed to happen more
clearly. How could she possibly say no?

CHAPTER FOUR

WHO WOULD HAVE THOUGHT?

Max had certainly never expected to be here, in the Christmas grotto of Cheltenham's largest department store. Or to be in sole charge of three small children, for that matter, but it seemed that things were going well on this outing. They had been going surprisingly well for the whole day, so far, in fact. He had wrangled the three different sizes of safety seats into his vehicle, figured out how to operate the three-wheeled mountain buggy for Alice and had taken the children on a drive to find a service station that hadn't run out of Christmas trees yet, after deciding that taking the children into the patch of forest on their property and trying to saw off large branches probably wasn't the most sensible idea. It was only after he had tied the tree securely to the roof rack of his Jeep and was planning to head back home to Upper Barnsley that Ben had informed him of the next Christmas 'rule', which was a visit to tell Father Christmas what they hoped would be their special gift this year.

So, here they were. Father Christmas, resplendent in red suit with white faux fur edging to match his luxuriant beard and the trimmings on his hat, was sitting on a large red velvet-covered chair with a golden edging. Christmas carols were playing softly in the background and the store staff were wearing red hats or headbands with glowing yellow stars. There were Christmas trees with twinkling lights and fake snow on either side of the chair, giant teddy bears, burlap sacks with the corners of pretend gifts peeping out and a life-sized reindeer that had a round red nose and a mouth curved into a rather unlikely smile. It was everything that Max had dismissed about Christmas for as long as he could remember.

Commercial hype. Children begged their parents to bring them here and there would be plenty of other shopping that needed to be done at the same time. Max could see the stoic expressions on some of the parents' faces already as they kept their places in the queue of over-excited children who were waiting their turn to whisper their secret Christmas wishes into the ear of the man who could make it happen. The children standing close to Max weren't over-excited, however. Ben and Tilly were standing very quietly, holding hands, beside the buggy in which Alice was soundly asleep for the moment. Too quietly, Max decided, looking around at the shining faces of other children and the way they were bouncing on their toes, barely able to contain themselves, when it was nearly their turn.

'What are you going to ask Father Christmas for?' he asked Ben.

Ben gave him a patient look. 'It's secret,' he said. 'It's—'

'—a rule,' Max said at the same time. He smiled at Ben. 'I get it.' He wondered if there was any way he could manage to stand close enough to overhear the request, however. Because how else was he going to know what he could get as Christmas gifts for his nephew and nieces?

They moved up the queue a little and Max let his gaze roam away from the grotto towards the strategically placed aisles of every kind of decoration you might want for your house or tree. During a breakfast that was still chaotic even though Maggie had arrived not long after Emma had left for the hospital, he'd told James about his decision to buy a Christmas tree and he'd been on the point of suggesting that they already had all the decorations they could possibly need, boxed up and stored in the attic. It was instantly obvious that his dad knew exactly what he was thinking about and it was just as clear that he wanted to avoid that discussion at all costs. The haunted look in his eyes was swiftly followed by excusing himself to go into the clinic rooms to get ready for a morning surgery followed by house calls.

'You know what?' Max said to Ben.

'What?'

'I think we're going to have a new Christmas rule this year. One that's just for us.'

The deep crease that appeared on Ben's forehead made his glance even more suspicious.

'Only if you think it's a good one,' Max added gravely. 'I reckon you know more about the rules than me.'

Ben considered this and then nodded his agreement. 'What is it?' he asked.

'Well…we've bought a new Christmas tree, haven't we?'

'Yes.'

'And we need to put things on it to look pretty, yes?'

'Stars…' Tilly was listening to the conversation. 'Emma said we can make stars and I can help.'

'I know.' Max had the sudden thought that maybe he might have a word in the ear of Father Christmas himself when they got close enough. So that he could put in a request that Emma would stay in the house for the next week at least. She hadn't exactly said yes when he'd asked her last night. But she hadn't said no either, so he hadn't given up hope. 'I'm sure she will,' he reassured Tilly.

'Emma is not the kind of person who would break a promise. But I was thinking that we might need something else to go with the stars. Something special that you guys can choose all by yourselves. After you've had your photo with Father Christmas.'

Ben was still frowning. 'But why is that a new rule?'

'Because we'll do it every Christmas,' Max told him quietly. 'And that means we'll always have special decorations to go on the tree that you know are yours because you chose them.'

Would the message beneath his words that Max only recognised himself as he was saying them be understood on some level by the children? That he was trying to make a promise that they were safe now and that he would do everything in his power to ensure that there weren't going to be any more huge and traumatic changes in their lives? It seemed to have helped a little, because Tilly's face was starting to look like the other little girls in this line. Her eyes were almost shining.

'Fairies,' she whispered. 'I like fairies.'

'I'll help you find a fairy,' Max said. 'Maybe one that can go right on the tippy top of the tree?'

They were getting closer to the front of the queue now and they were all watching as a small girl was lifted onto Father Christmas's knee. He tilted his head and she cupped her hands around her mouth to keep her wish secret and then beamed at her mother, who was standing beside the photographer. Noticing that the mother's purse was already open so that she could purchase the image should have scored another point for the commercialism that Max detested but, oddly, it didn't. What he could see was the love in this mother's face, her pleasure in having brought her daughter to the Christmas grotto and the sheer joy in the little girl's face.

And he remembered something else then. From the time before he had learned to dismiss everything about Christmas. He remembered being taken to see Father Christmas when he wouldn't have been much older than Ben. With Andy, who would have been about Tilly's age. And their mother had been watching them with love written all over *her* face and…and…

And he could remember the magic. The belief that the man in the red suit could make something special happen. He could also remember that belief becoming something even bigger when he'd come downstairs on Christmas morning to find the gift he'd set his heart on underneath the tree—his first two-wheeler bike with red tinsel wrapped all over it. His wish had come true and it was the best thing *ever*.

Look at that… His mother had the biggest smile on her face as she stood there wrapped in his father's arms. *I wonder how Father Christmas got that down the chimney?*

Max had known. By magic. And even though he knew perfectly well now that it had been his parents who'd put the bike there, he also knew that there had been magic involved. The kind of magic that Emma had been talking about in the bonds within a family. About the sharing and celebration and joy. And she had been right about something else too. These particular children needed to find new bonds that they could trust enough to feel safe and they needed a particularly special Christmas this year.

But he needed help to make that happen. From someone who knew far more about children than he did. Someone who knew more about families than he did and who was warm and caring enough to be able to encourage the connections that would lead to bonds that could form and then get stronger and stronger.

'Do you want to go and visit Emma after we're finished here?' he asked Ben and Tilly. 'It's not far away to where she's working in my hospital. If we find out what she needs to help you make stars, we could pick that up on the way home.'

Emma's first thought when she came out of a curtained cubicle and saw Max Cunningham coming into the emergency department of the Royal with the three children in tow was that something was wrong. Her heart skipped a beat as she imagined one of the children was ill or injured and that must have shown in her face as she walked towards them because Max was smiling reassuringly.

More than reassuringly, actually. He was smiling at Emma as if she was the person he most wanted to see in the world and her body was responding with that glow of warmth and funny tingling thing that went down to her toes. It was impossible not to smile back. Or to hold the gaze of those amazingly blue eyes. He'd always been a very good-looking man but ageing ten years had added a maturity that was even more appealing. It wasn't hard to stamp on her body's response, though, and tell herself how stupid it would be to entertain any ideas of Max being aware of any physical reactions to *her* proximity. She only had to remember how he'd laughed after that kiss. How quick he'd been to reassure her.

'Don't worry, Emma, you're completely safe. We both know you're so not my type and I'm certainly not yours...'

She'd laughed along with him, albeit a heartbeat later. He was right. What woman in her right mind would willingly go near someone who was guaranteed to break their heart if they were silly enough to fall for him?

Her smile was fading as the memory flashed through the back of her mind but Max was still beaming at her.

'We just came in to say hullo,' he said. 'I wondered how things were going?'

'Everything's great,' Emma assured him. 'It was quiet enough first thing for me to get to know my way around and meet most of the staff. Miriam's been amazingly helpful.'

The senior nurse was making a beeline for the group as she was speaking.

'Emma's a complete pro,' she told Max. 'I doubt there's anything she couldn't cope with.' But Miriam's attention was on the children and she automatically reached into the buggy to unclip and pick up the baby as Alice began to whimper. 'May I?'

'Please do,' Max said. 'But she's due for a nappy change and a bottle. We've been busy visiting Father Christmas in Derby's department store.'

'Just the sort of thing a grandma is expert in,' Miriam responded, as she gathered

Alice into her arms. 'Is everything in that bag there?'

'She's hungry,' Ben told Miriam.

'I think you're right, lovey. And what about you? We've got some lovely Christmas cookies in our staffroom that look like snowmen. Would you like to come and have some?'

Ben nodded solemnly and Emma had to smile as she saw Tilly's hand slide into his. If her big brother was going to get cookies, she wanted to go too.

Max was still smiling as he watched Miriam take Ben's hand to lead both the older children towards the staffroom.

'You look like you're having a good day,' she said.

'So far, so good.' Max nodded. 'I did want to get close enough to hear what Ben and Tilly were asking Father Christmas for but it didn't work.' He raised an eyebrow at Emma. 'Maybe you could find out? I'd really like to put something special under the tree for them both.'

Was he expecting her to be heading back to the Cunningham house after work? It was only then that Emma realised she hadn't made any effort to look for alternative accommodation yet. She'd been far too focused on her work in this new emergency department. She could find out, she thought. She could help the children write a letter to Father Christmas, maybe, to put into the fire so it went up the chimney. If she promised to keep their secrets, they might tell her exactly what to write.

'Oh, we got a tree too,' Max continued. 'And they both chose some decorations to go on it. Ben got a box of tin soldiers and Tilly chose an angel to go on top of the tree—although she thinks it's a fairy.' His gaze was roaming around his department over Emma's shoulder. 'So...have you had any excitement?'

'Not really. We've only used a resuscitation room once, for a serious stroke that came in early this morning. Apart from that, it's been the usual range of problems like chest pain and asthma and some diabetes complications. There was an interesting tib/fib fracture, though...it—'

But Max obviously wasn't listening. His

gaze was fixed behind Emma. About where the first set of automatic doors to the ambulance bay were.

'Something's happening,' he interrupted her.

Emma turned swiftly to see someone standing outside the outer doors that needed a code to open. It was a man who had a child in his arms and, even from this distance, Emma could see that the child was bleeding heavily. One of the two paramedics who were using the space between the sets of doors to finish some paperwork and clean a stretcher moved to press the button that would open the doors at the same time as both Emma and Max had moved close enough for the inner doors to slide open.

'There's more.' The man carrying the injured child was out of breath and sounded panicked. 'Out on the main road. A truck just smashed into about three parked cars. They need help...'

Another ED consultant was right behind Max and Emma.

'I'll take him,' she said. 'Do you want me to activate the trauma team as well?'

'Yes.'

Both Emma and Max spoke at the same time and she had the immediate thought that perhaps she should let Max take charge of this emergency, even though, technically, she was here to do his job. He must have felt her swift glance because he caught her gaze and he clearly wasn't thinking about whether or not he was even supposed to be there.

'We'd better get out there,' he said. 'We're needed.'

Emma hadn't been waiting for his direction. She was already heading for the outer doors despite being in her scrubs, with nothing more than a long-sleeved tee shirt underneath the tunic.

'I'll get our kit,' one of the paramedics said. He turned to his partner. 'You bring the truck so we can transport more quickly.'

Glancing back into the department as the child was carried inside for assessment and treatment, Emma saw Max hesitating for a brief moment before he followed her and he too was looking back into the department. Towards the staffroom where Miriam had taken the children to give them cookies? Emma could sense that he was struggling with something different this time. Not who should take charge of this incident but with his new responsibilities as a father figure clashing with what he was programmed to respond to as an emergency physician. Was this another reminder of just how much his life was changing? His next words confirmed her line of thought.

'Tell Miriam where I am,' he called after his colleague. 'Ask her to keep an eye on the children for me?'

And then they were outside and running towards the scene that lay just out of the hospital grounds, in the direction that Emma had taken only yesterday when she'd walked with Max to see his apartment. The same intersection where they'd waited for the traffic lights to change and she'd noticed the impressive overhead decorations of icicle lights. Any thought of pretty things to do with Christmas was totally incongruous at this moment, however. It looked as though a large truck had failed to notice the line of stationary cars waiting at a red light and had smashed into the end of the line, in a nose-to-tail concertina of at least three vehicles that suggested a great deal of speed had been involved. The truck had tipped sideways with the impact and there was another vehicle almost hidden beneath the body of the truck.

Emma had seen plenty of road traffic accidents over the years but nothing quite like this. There was a crowd gathering, with people trying to get into vehicles where doors had been crushed and couldn't open. They must have come from the lines of traffic now building up in a traffic jam on all sides of the intersection because many of them looked deserted, with doors hanging open. There were flashing lights and sirens coming from all directions as emergency service vehicles rushed to the scene but, even over all that noise, Emma could hear the cries of frightened people. Her steps slowed as she got closer to the carnage and—although Max had been a step or two ahead of her the whole time they'd been running—he seemed to sense the distance between them increasing and he also slowed, turning back to catch her gaze.

'You okay, Em?'

She nodded, sucking in a deep, deep breath. She knew she had the skills to tackle a scene like this but, for this moment, it was overwhelming. The temptation to hang back and allow Max to take the lead was strong but there was something equally strong and that was a hard-won determination to face up to the most difficult things life could throw at her and Emma wasn't about to throw away any part of her confidence in being able to do that successfully.

Max was still holding her gaze and it felt as if he could sense that momentary doubt. As if he was having a similar one of his own, even, and wondering if he should take the lead.

'We're right beside the hospital,' she said, turning her head now to survey the scene and assess the dangers and where they might be needed as a priority. 'All we need to do at this point is to make sure they're stable enough to get them inside. Basics. Airway, breathing, circulation. Look after the cervical spine. We've got lots of help. The firies will cut into the vehicles for us if it's needed. The paramedics can direct the extrication and transfer.'

'Here…' A paramedic was coming towards them. 'Put these on.'

'These' were fluorescent vests with the word 'Doctor' on the back on a reflective strip.

'No…hang on…' A female paramedic was pulling off her jacket, which she handed to Emma. 'You're going to freeze in scrubs. Put this on first.'

'But what about you?'

'I've got something else I can wear.'

'Has anybody started triage?' Max asked.

'We've only just got here. That's our MCI command vehicle arriving now, behind the fire truck.'

Emma knew that MCI stood for Mass Casualty Incident. She looked at the line of crushed vehicles. Should they start at the front and work back? One of the cars was sandwiched between one in front and one behind and it looked as though the damage in that case was worse than the others. But what about the vehicle beneath the overturned truck?

Max clearly wanted to start the work that urgently needed to be done here. Emma shoved her arms into the warm jacket.

'Have you got triage labels?'

The paramedic who'd opened the ambulance bay doors of the Royal to let in the man with the injured child was beside Emma now. 'I've got them,' he said. 'Can you come with me? We'll do a first sweep and if you're both with me, I can leave you to start treating any red labels and move on. We still don't know what we're dealing with in terms of numbers or severity of injuries.'

Emma had worked with the triage labelling system as well. A red label meant that the victim could only survive with immediate treatment. They might have an obstructed airway or rate of respiration that was far too slow or fast, a very rapid heart rate or an absent radial pulse indicating low blood pressure, potentially from severe blood loss.

The first car in the line had been shunted well into the intersection. There were by-standers clustered around the driver's side of the car. The window was broken and Emma could see the deflated airbag hanging from the steering wheel.

'She's awake,' someone told them. 'She says her neck hurts and she doesn't want to try moving.'

She was conscious, breathing and talking so this driver wasn't going to get a red label indicating the need for urgent intervention to save a life. A potential neck injury could still be serious but it could wait.

'Tell her to keep as still as possible,' the paramedic instructed. 'Someone will be with her very soon.'

They moved swiftly to the next vehicle. The paramedic was using his radio to relay information to the person who was taking charge of the scene and would use the available resources of people and equipment according to information coming in and any changes during the operation. Police officers were on scene now, as well, moving by-standers out of the way and trying to clear the blocked traffic.

There were two people inside the second vehicle, both conscious.

'It's my leg,' the front seat passenger groaned. 'I think it's broken.'

The driver was only semi-conscious. 'Where am I?' she mumbled. 'What's happened?'

More paramedics had arrived on scene and were immediately dispatched to manage these patients.

It was the third car in the line that was the most seriously damaged, apart from the one beneath the truck, and it was rapidly, sadly clear that there was nothing they could do for this woman. Her black triage label was a sombre confirmation that the rescue teams were not needed.

'Maybe if we'd got here a bit faster?' Emma said.

But Max shook his head. 'Unsurvivable injuries. I suspect the force from behind and the weight of obstruction in front was enough to just snap her neck.'

A fire crew was close and had a tarpaulin to put over the car containing the fatality.

'Truck driver seems uninjured,' they told Emma and Max. 'Got himself out of the cab. The cops are having a word with him.'

'I'll go and check him out.' The paramedic's tone was carefully neutral. It was obvious that the truck driver was responsible for this horrific crash that had killed at least one person but they couldn't make judgements about the driver involved. It was possible that it was a medical event or mechanical failure that had caused him to hit a line of stationary vehicles at high speed.

The fire crew was also making decisions about how to get to the car trapped beneath the truck and Emma heard someone talking about stabilising the truck until they could get the machinery they needed to lift it clear. Looking at how crushed the car was, with its roof almost down past the level of the steering wheel, she fully expected that the driver would be another fatality. She bent to try and look through the front window on the passenger's side.

'Careful, there, Doc,' one of the fire officers shouted. 'We're not sure how stable it is.'

The call was enough to have Max by her side instantly and it felt as though he was there to try and protect her. He was certainly ready to assist. Or did he want to take over?

'What can you see?'

'Facial injuries. I can't see any chest wall movement...' Emma had her bottom lip caught between her teeth as she scanned the driver's body as best she could. The seat had been flattened by the roof being crushed so he was lying almost flat, still wearing his seat belt. She couldn't see any major bleeding other than the injury to his face but... 'Oh...' Emma felt her heart skip a beat. 'I *can* see chest wall movement. He's breathing. Or trying to...'

Max had his head right beside hers now, as he tried to get a visual assessment of the crash victim. He was so close she could feel the warmth of his skin and, like the way he'd looked at her when they'd first arrived on this scene, it seemed that just being close to him was empowering Emma with more confidence than she'd ever known she had.

She turned to the fire crew. 'I have to get in here,' she said. 'It's urgent.'

'We're still assessing how stable this truck is. We can't start cutting the car up for access until we've got jacks in place or lifted the chassis clear.'

'There's no time for that.' Emma shook her head. 'Can you break this back window? I reckon I could get in there.'

'There's hardly any space in there.' The paramedic had come back. 'There's no way we could get a spinal board in and get him out.'

Both the paramedic and Max were tall, broad-shouldered men. They wouldn't even be able to get through a window space. But Emma could—if she was brave enough. Again, as she had when first arriving on this scene, she had a moment of wondering if she might be about to tackle something that might defeat her. And, again, she found herself catching Max's gaze. This time, it felt different. He wasn't considering taking over because he couldn't do what Emma could attempt, thanks to her size. This time, it felt as if he was offering her encouragement. Bolstering her confidence by letting her know that he believed she could do this. And it felt...great. It was exactly what she needed to vanquish any beat of fear.

'I can get in,' she told them. 'I need to secure his airway. I can work in a tight space. You could pass me in the gear I need.' She had to try and save this man. He'd been simply sitting in his car, stopped at a red traffic light, and his world had just been overturned in a split second and it just...well, it wasn't fair...

The chief fire officer looked undecided but Emma held his gaze to give him the silent message if he wasn't going to help her, she was going to try by herself.

He finally nodded. 'Okay. Stand back and I'll get the window out.'

He should go back to his emergency department, Max thought. It wasn't just that he'd left all the children in the care of a staff member.

He was automatically focusing on how the department was going to cope with a sudden influx of trauma patients. He knew that his staff would be managing the first of these patients from the crash scene perfectly well, but the more seriously injured, like the semi-conscious driver of the second vehicle, might be stretching immediate resources and they needed to plan for someone who could need major resuscitation—if they could get him into the department alive. Or maybe it should be Emma who went back to manage the department, seeing as she was officially doing his job today.

But right now she was wriggling herself through an empty window space of a crashed car and somehow contorting her body so that she could touch and assess the unconscious driver. She was inside a partially crushed car and there was a heavy truck still lying across the vehicle. It looked difficult and bloody dangerous and…and there was no way Max was going to leave until he knew that Emma was okay. He couldn't believe the courage she'd shown even crawling into that vehicle.

The fact that she now sounded calm and in control of the situation was, well…it was seriously impressive.

'He's got multiple fractures in his face and his airway's obstructed.' Emma put down the bag mask she had been trying to use to assist the man's breathing. 'There's no way I'm going to be able to do an orotracheal or nasotracheal intubation. How far away are we from being able to get him out?'

Max signalled one of the fire officers and repeated Emma's query.

'We're getting some jacks in place. It should be safe enough to cut the side out of the car in about ten minutes.'

Emma had heard the response. 'Too long,' she said. She was almost lying down beside her patient in the narrow space left in the crushed car but she twisted her head to look directly at Max.

'Surgical cricothyroidotomy?' she suggested.

'It's what I'd do in ED.' He nodded. 'But have you got enough space in there?'

'It'll have to be enough,' Emma said. 'His

pulse is dropping. We're going to lose him if I don't do something right now. I need some fresh gloves, a number ten or eleven scalpel, a bougie and a size six endotracheal tube, please.'

It was Max who handed everything that Emma required in through the empty window space, reaching in so that he could place things in her hands without her having to try and move. With her new gloves on, he watched her find her landmarks on the man's neck, stabilising the larynx with one hand and then locating the space between the thyroid and cricoid cartilages. He was ready to hand her the scalpel as soon as she was ready to make her first incision.

'I'm through the cricoid membrane,' she said, seconds later. 'I'm going to make the horizontal incisions now.'

Max knew this was where things could get messy and enough blood could not only obscure the field but undermine the confidence of anyone who might not be very familiar with this emergency procedure. He knew that Emma was going to be working purely by feel from now on and when there was movement of the crushed vehicle from what the firies were doing to stabilise the truck above them, he held his breath to see whether that might give Emma enough of a fright to interfere with what was the critical moment of her attempt to save this man's life.

It didn't seem to rattle her at all. She slid the bougie guide into the hole she'd made in his neck, slipped the endotracheal tube over the top of the bougie and managed to make it look easy to secure the tube, despite the awkwardness of the space she was working in and gloved hands that were slippery with blood.

'Can you see where the bag mask is?' she asked Max.

'It's right behind you.'

'I can't reach…'

'I've got it.' Max leaned further into the car and picked it up. He pulled off the plastic face mask and the paramedic beside him had the attachment needed so that Emma could clip it to the endotracheal tube.

'Equal chest movement,' she said a moment

later. 'Can we get some oxygen on? I'd like to get an IV in, as well.'

Max could see the firies setting up their hydraulic cutting gear right beside him. As he looked at the officer in charge he received a nod in response.

'They're ready to start cutting,' he told Emma. 'Is he breathing well enough to wait a couple of minutes until we can get him out? The sooner we can get him into the department the better, yes?'

'Of course.' Emma had one hand on the man's abdomen, feeling for his efforts at respiration. She had her other hand on his wrist, feeling for his pulse. 'Okay…yes…let's get him out of here.'

She stayed with her patient for as long as possible as the firies cut through twisted metal and lifted a door and the central pillar out of the way. Then she had to move and the paramedics took over, being the experts in getting the victim onto a spinal board and then out of the vehicle and onto the waiting stretcher. It took only a few minutes but, for that period of time, Max had Emma standing right beside him and he could sense her focus on what was happening for her patient and a tension that suggested that a successful outcome to this case was very, very important to her.

He was looking at her face as the badly injured man was finally lifted from the car and, as if sensing his gaze, she looked up at him and he could see what he had suspected in her eyes. Emma was determined to win this fight for life. She not only had a bucket of courage, this woman, but she loved her job as much as Max loved his and she truly cared about doing the absolute best she could for anyone under her care. It was a moment of connection that was as powerful as it was brief.

Their patient had been freed but needed more intervention and then a high level of monitoring even for the few minutes it would take to get him inside the hospital walls. The other victims of this incident had already been transported into the Royal's emergency department and that was where Emma and Max both headed back to now. There was still a lot of work to be done and Max wanted to be working alongside Emma to make sure the department could handle everything that needed to be done for everybody involved.

It was then he realised that, during the tense minutes of assisting Emma in the amazing job she'd just done in saving a man's life, he'd actually forgotten that he had other responsibilities as well. That there were three small children waiting for him, probably in the staffroom of his emergency department. He felt completely torn in that moment—in two very different directions—and it was overwhelming.

Had Emma sensed that it was almost too much? Was that why she chose to look up from her patient for a heartbeat and catch his gaze? There was a softness to her mouth that hinted at a smile and there was a confidence in her eyes that told him she thought they were winning. That they had a very good chance of winning this challenge they had just tackled together.

Max chose to take something more from that look as well. That he might well be facing the biggest challenge of his own life but he had a very good chance of winning that too. Especially if he could persuade Emma to hang around, even if was only for a short time. And then he remembered that was why he had dropped by the hospital in the first place—to try and persuade her not to find alternative accommodation.

He'd have to wait before he could find an appropriate moment to do that so he hoped the children were happy to stay for a bit longer. That would also give him time to think up an approach that Emma couldn't refuse.

He could remind her of her promise to help Ben and Tilly make stars.

Or he could remind her of what she believed about Christmas. About the magic that could happen when a family came together to celebrate the bonds they had. The love. He could tell her what he believed—that they all needed Emma to make that happen.

CHAPTER FIVE

THIS FELT AS if it could be a mistake.

As if Emma was doing something that meant she was stepping over a line and it might be impossible to step back again even if she really needed to. But here she was, doing it. Driving back to Upper Barnsley. And it was Max Cunningham's fault.

He had made it impossible for her not to return to the manor house after her shift had ended. He had stayed on at the Royal, allowing staff members to take care of his nieces and nephew, until they had stabilised all the victims of the major accident and their patients had been transferred either to Theatre under the care of surgical teams or admitted to various wards for further treatment.

And then he'd brought the children in from the staffroom or the relatives' room or wherever someone had been caring for them and Ben had pinned Emma with that gaze that was far too serious for a six-year-old boy to have mastered.

'Is it time for you to go home now, Emma?' he'd asked.

'I guess it is,' she'd admitted, checking her watch. But just where it was that she would be heading as her temporary home was totally unknown. She hadn't found a single moment today to go online and check for the availability of hotel rooms within a manageable distance.

'Are we going to make stars?' Tilly's gaze was almost as sombre as her brother's—as if she was still processing her new knowledge that life didn't always deliver what it was supposed to. 'I like stars and...and you said I could help.'

Ben still had her pinned. 'You promised...'

Technically, Emma had offered rather than promised to show the children how to make stars but the semantics were irrelevant because she couldn't let Ben and Tilly down.

Or Max...

If he'd brought these children in to see her as a form of emotional blackmail to get another night of her assistance with their care, he had certainly achieved his goal but that wasn't what Emma was thinking about as her gaze touched, and then held, his.

To be honest, she wasn't thinking of anything very coherent at all. It was more of a feeling. A warmth. They had worked together this afternoon. They had saved a life and the connection that gave them was more than simply professional. They had shared a goal and they'd needed each other in order to achieve it and they had succeeded and… trust between them had been born. It was that trust that was creating a warmth that started in Emma's chest and unfurled and grew to reach right to the tips of her fingers and toes.

Or maybe the connection had already been there from years ago and had been rediscovered.

And maybe a new depth to that connection had been established between them yesterday when Emma had been present while Max was struggling to get his head around the enormous changes that had just overturned his world. She had helped because she was there and she couldn't *not* help but then he'd asked her to stay. He'd said that he *needed* her...

Whatever it was, it was powerful. And it was touching something very deep in Emma's heart. Not in the space that was still locked away because she didn't quite recognise this new part of her heart. It felt like no-man's land, halfway between caring so much that something could tear your heart apart when you lost it and caring only because you knew that it was temporary so the loss was already built in—the now very familiar space that her locum work had given her in her professional life and the avoidance of any long-term relationships had provided in her private life.

For a moment, Emma had to shake off a longing that came completely from left field—that she was over being in this space and ready to put roots down and create a life that wasn't going to keep changing. As always, the best way to deal with a doubt like that was to think of a positive point to balance it and there was one that sprang to mind instantly. It almost felt as if she could allow herself to enjoy the sensations that came from unwrapping an old attraction that didn't seem to have faded at all because this was as temporary as her new position being the stand-in HOD of the Royal's emergency department. She knew that when this locum position ended she would walk out of the job and away from Max Cunningham and his now very complicated life would be none of her business. Perhaps she could even allow herself to enjoy the company of young children—away from her professional environment—which was something she knew she had instinctively kept herself away from.

It was all temporary. Keeping her word to show Ben and Tilly how to make stars committed her to no more than spending one more night at the manor house. She could find the time to search for a hotel room tomorrow.

Pulling her car to a halt beside Max's, outside his family home, Emma sat still for a moment, watching Max get out of the driver's seat and move to open the back door to lift his small passengers from their car seats. He paused for a heartbeat, however, and looked over the Christmas tree strapped to the roof of the vehicle to catch Emma's gaze, his lips curling into a smile.

Emma's breath came out in a sigh that held the edge of an unexpected sound.

Oh, yeah…that attraction hadn't faded at all. It seemed to have matured into something that had rather a lot more bite to it and she recognised the tiny sound that had escaped with her breath for what it was—an expression of physical desire.

Lust, even…

It had been a weird thing to think about as he unclipped Tilly's safety belt and lifted her from her car seat but there was no way that Max could have stopped the memory filling his head.

That time he'd kissed Emma Moretti under the mistletoe at the paediatric ward's staff Christmas party. He hadn't given it any more thought after it had happened because, no matter how soft her lips had been and how delicious the curves of her body were and how astonishingly powerful the urge to do a lot more than kiss Emma had been, it was never going to happen.

Emma was the earth mother type. The type who was destined to marry and have a family as soon as possible. A huge family, probably, seeing as she had adored children and babies so much and, because that was something Max wanted to avoid at all costs, it had been easy to dismiss the attraction that had both led to and been inflamed by that kiss.

Dismissing it hadn't made it go away, though, had it? Judging by the kick in his gut that Max recognised all too easily as a reaction to a very healthy physical attraction, it was actually stronger than it had ever been.

Was that because there were things about Emma that were familiar but other things that were so very different? She was just as gorgeous as she'd been ten years ago, even though she was less curvy and she had cut off those glorious long waves of her hair and she seemed…what was it, exactly? More contained, perhaps? Less ready to laugh or even smile. Yes, she was definitely different but that gave the attraction an edge of mystery that added surprisingly to its power.

Emma wasn't the only one who was different, either. Who could have predicted that he'd be the one who'd end up with what seemed a huge family and the earth mother would still be alone?

He set Tilly down on her feet beside Ben, who immediately took hold of his sister's hand, and then he unclipped the bucket seat that Alice was strapped into.

'Okay, guys. Let's go inside and say hullo to Grandpa and then I'll bring the Christmas tree inside.'

But James Cunningham was nowhere to be seen. Neither was their housekeeper, Maggie, though she'd left a note in the kitchen with a list of food she had prepared for both the children and adults.

'Dad's probably in the clinic. Or on a house call. Or he might have taken Pirate for a walk.'

Or he might be avoiding spending time

with his grandchildren because, like Max, he was still grappling with how to cope with his new responsibilities.

Alice had begun to cry as they'd come inside. Max had a brief but fierce yearning for the old days in the paediatric ward when he'd been working with Emma and how he had been able to hand a baby back to its mother or a nurse when it needed changing or feeding, but he wasn't about to repeat his actions of the previous evening of shoving Alice into Emma's arms.

Not when he had been quite aware of that flash of something like panic he'd seen in her eyes, even as her arms had gathered the baby close. Besides, he had to learn how to cope and this was as good a time as any. He pulled wipes and a clean nappy from the bag of supplies he had taken into town earlier and set about making Alice comfortable. It was a mission to deal with all those fiddly little fasteners on her stretchy suit and clean that tiny bottom when she was kicking her legs so energetically and by the time he carried the baby into the kitchen to get on with his next task of preparing a bottle of formula he found Emma sitting at the long table with an array of materials in front of her that included all the cardboard boxes she had gathered at the hospital before coming home.

She was cutting a shape from the cardboard as Max held Alice with one arm and used his free hand to measure scoops of formula into a bottle the way Maggie had shown him yesterday.

'So this will be a big star,' Emma told Ben and Tilly. 'And I'll make a shape for a small star, as well. You can trace around them on other pieces of cardboard and then I can help you cut them out.'

'I can cut things out all by myself,' Ben said.

'Me too,' said Tilly.

Emma's nod was apologetic. 'Of course you can,' she said. 'But I can help if you want me to. And when we've cut some out, I'll show you how to cover them with the silver foil. And then we need to make a hole in one of the pointy bits.'

'Why?'

'So we can tie the stars to the tree. I'm sure we can find some string somewhere.'

Ben looked up at Max as he shook the bottle to dissolve the formula in the cooled boiled water. 'Did you bring the tree inside, Uncle Max?'

'Not yet, Ben. But I will, just as soon as I give Alice her dinner.' He tested the temperature of the milk against his wrist and hoped that how confident he'd just sounded was justified. He still hadn't managed to get Alice to accept a bottle from him yet. Last night he'd needed Emma to rescue him. Maggie had been on hand this morning and Miriam, along with other staff members, had been only too happy to take over when he'd taken the children into work.

Max was holding his breath as he took a seat at the far end of the kitchen table, tipped Alice back into the crook of his elbow and offered her the teat of the bottle as her hungry whimpers became more frantic. He saw the startled expression on her face as she looked up at this new person trying to feed her but she had already tasted the milk and hunger seemed to win the battle with any lack of trust. Her lips closed around the teat and her tiny hands came up to help Max hold the bottle as she began to suck.

He knew he was smiling as he looked up to see if Emma had witnessed this triumph. Max felt absurdly proud of himself. So much so, he actually had a bit of a lump in his throat. He could do this. He *was* doing it.

Emma had a rather oddly shaped cardboard star in her hands and she was showing the children how to wrap it in silver foil but she must have been watching Max's efforts with Alice from the corner of her eye because she caught his gaze as the contented silence of the baby continued and her smile only made him feel even prouder.

Emma was impressed.

And then something weird happened.

It was like one of those photographs where the image had been captured from multiple cameras surrounding the group or one that had been created during that mannequin challenge that had gone viral where everybody froze in the middle of doing something. The effect was that Max was suddenly and acutely aware of so many tiny things, all at once.

There was the weight and warmth of the baby in his arms and the feather-light touch of those miniature fingers against his own hands. He could smell the combination of the milk she was drinking and the baby smell that was partly shampoo and lotion but something else that was just unique to babies, or maybe to this particular baby. He could also see the older children. Ben was standing beside Emma, leaning on her arm as he watched what she was doing with absolute concentration. Tilly had somehow wriggled onto Emma's lap to get closer to the action but she wasn't watching the foil being folded around the points of the cardboard star—she was looking up at Emma.

And Emma, well, she was looking at Max and, while the scene couldn't actually be any more different to the drama of the rescue scene this afternoon when Emma was folded inside that wreck of a car and he was assisting her with that life-saving intervention, there was something similar in this connection. They were a team and, in this moment of time, they were succeeding in what they were trying to achieve.

But there was more to it than that. A whole lot more.

This… Max had to swallow the lump in his throat that had just become oddly uncomfortable. This was a *family* moment and it took him back in time. To when he still had his younger brother in his life. And the mother he had adored so much. A time when they might well have been doing something together, in this very kitchen. A time when this house had been such a happy place. A real home…

Suddenly—shockingly—Max could see right through that barrier he'd started creating as a young boy. The barrier that made him believe that he never really wanted what he'd once had as part of a loving family. That life would be far less painful and much more fun if he just skated across the surface when it came to relationships with other people. If he could turn away from things that were so big they were terrifying and he could simply shut them away in a place he never really needed to visit.

He became the son who loved his father very much but never strayed into the private, sad space that James Cunningham had retreated to after his beloved wife's death.

A big brother who thought he was being kind by telling Andy that Father Christmas didn't exist and that they needed to grow up and look after themselves so that they didn't make things worse for their father.

An uncle who was quite happy to play with the members of a new generation of the Cunningham family but was never tempted by the idea of having children of his own.

A lover who could recognise the moment a woman was falling in love with him and wanted more and took the first opportunity to end things as kindly, but finally, as possible.

And, in this rather shocking moment, he could see that behind those barriers was someone who actually, desperately wanted precisely the things he had spent a lifetime protecting himself from. He wanted the kind of committed, loving relationship his parents had had. He wanted to watch his children grow up. To protect and guide them.

To love them. To have a partner by his side who would also love his children. Who would love *him* and choose to be with him for the rest of her life.

Someone like… Emma…?

As if she had sensed that astonishing thought, Emma broke the eye contact with Max.

'It's your turn now, Ben,' she said. 'You can put the silver foil on the star you cut out.'

Max could have smiled at the wonky star with rather round points that Ben had made but he didn't. It was partly because he wouldn't have wanted to hurt Ben's feelings but it was more to do with the shock of that insight and the idea that he might have got things terribly wrong all those years ago. Thankfully, he could sense those barriers becoming rapidly cloudy again so that he was losing the impression of what he'd seen behind them. He had taught himself well to push those things that were emotionally too big to deal with into the space where they could be locked away.

He might be being forced to have the family he'd never imagined he'd ever have, but that didn't mean he had to take the risk of including anyone else in his life. Good grief...he only had to remember Andy's anguish when his marriage had failed to know that trusting the romantic kind of love was even more of a risk than opening your heart to being a loving father figure. He'd never know whether driving into that tree at high speed had really been accidental but the grief from his brother's death had been devastating enough anyway. He'd lost half his family now. A bit more than that, perhaps, because his father had never been the same since his mother had died so he'd lost a part of him as well.

It was too much loss for anyone.

Max let his breath out in a sigh of relief as Alice finished the last drops of her milk. He set the bottle on the table and moved Alice so that she was upright against his shoulder and he could rub her back to encourage a burp. That barrier was solid again, he realised. He

was safe. Maybe it was partly that relief that
made him turn his head so that he could press
a soft kiss to that silky baby hair. Okay, the
barrier had clearly shifted a little and he knew
he could make space for these children in his
heart. But that was all. His father had never
recovered from losing the woman he'd given
his heart to and Max knew that the failure of
Andy's marriage had been the cause of his
death, whether it had been deliberate or simply the fact that he'd been so devastated it
had been enough to make him do something
he'd never have normally done and get behind
the wheel of a car when he was drunk. Marriage—or any kind of long-term commitment
to a partner—was still well off Max's radar.

Emma was as safe as he was from anything
more than a professional relationship and/or
friendship.

James Cunningham didn't approve of the
Christmas tree in the drawing room.

Not that he'd said anything, but Emma
could sense his shock when he'd walked in
when she was helping Ben tie his homemade

stars to the branches of the tree that Max had brought inside and set up on one side of the fireplace under Ben's direction.

'It has to be close to the chimney,' he'd told them. 'So that Father Christmas doesn't have to go looking for it. He doesn't have time to do that when he's got so many chimneys he has to go down.'

When James came into the room, Max was holding Tilly up to put her fairy/angel on the top of the tree and Emma had her arms around Ben, gently guiding his small fingers as he tried to tie a bow in the string that they had threaded through the hole in one point of his star.

Max's father had frozen—just for a heart-beat—and, for Emma, it felt as if the world stopped turning for that instant in time as well. She could see what James was seeing. A man with a small girl in his arms, smiling as he watched her stretch out to put the skirt of the angel over the uppermost branch of the tree. A woman almost cradling an older child and a baby asleep in a pram to one side. The fire was crackling softly beside them and it didn't matter that the small number of homemade silver stars, even with the tin soldiers Ben had chosen and the angel for the top of the tree that had been Tilly's choice, still left the tree looking virtually devoid of decorations—this was a snapshot of a family Christmas and all it needed now was the grandfather looking on from the comfort of his leather chair, with his cute dog at his feet.

And Emma could feel something expanding inside her chest. She knew it wasn't physically possible that her heart could be changing size but that was what it felt like. It was getting rapidly bigger. Too big, because it was starting to crack. And bleed...

This... This feeling of family and Christmas. Of having different generations coming together to celebrate something special. Of having children dependent on her for as much love and protection that she could offer and having a partner that she could share the journey with...

She still wanted this. She wanted it so badly it was making her heart ache as much as if it had really split open.

And, maybe, Max's father was aware of a similar sense of yearning. Or loss, perhaps. Because, after that single heartbeat of time, he turned on his heel, snapping his fingers for Pirate to follow him out of the room and his spoken words were only for his dog.

'Sorry,' he muttered. 'I forgot. It's time for your walk, boy.'

Pirate hesitated for a moment, as if he was also contemplating the scene in front of him and would rather stay, but then turned and followed his master out of the room.

Emma had to take her hands away from where they were touching Ben's because she knew that he would notice they were shaking. She needed to gulp in a breath of air as well, because it might have only been an instant in time but it felt like she hadn't taken a breath in quite a while.

This was exactly what she had feared might happen if she became any more involved with the Cunningham men and these children. That she would be reminded that she still didn't have what she'd wanted most in life for almost as long as she could remember—

to have a family of her own. She'd taught herself to live without it. To be okay with the idea that it might never happen, in fact, because the walls she had built around her heart and her new lifestyle of never being in one place for a long time had been how she'd coped so well for so long. But she was safe, because that wasn't about to change. Or not yet, anyway. Not when she would be leaving this part of the world in a matter of days. Not for children who belonged to another family or a man who'd never been interested in her.

Except...that wasn't quite true, was it?

He'd been interested enough to kiss her that one time.

And Emma was almost sure he remembered that kiss as well as she did. She also knew they'd both changed enough for curiosity to be part of a feeling of connection between them and...after the intense way Max had been looking at her over the top of the Christmas tree strapped to his car this afternoon, she had a sense that the increased attraction she was so aware of could very well be mutual.

She let out the breath she had taken slowly. A sexual attraction was completely different to the minefield of emotions that came with the notions of family and forever. That was something she could cope with, even if it wasn't something she'd included in her life for a very long time. And she didn't have to think about it right now because there were more important things to focus on.

'Good job, Ben,' she said aloud. 'That's a beautiful star.'

CHAPTER SIX

THE WALK WITH Pirate seemed to have given James whatever inner strength he needed to get back on track with coping and he helped with getting the children fed, bathed and into bed. He excused himself as he stood up from the kitchen table after dinner, however, to retire to his room instead of sitting by the fire.

'It's been a long day,' he said.

'You sure you don't want a nightcap?' Max asked. 'I'm going to have one. Emma? Would you like a glass of wine?'

'I would,' Emma said. 'Thank you.'

'You deserve a chance to wind down properly,' Max said as he went to the fridge to collect the bottle he'd opened the night before. 'You've had a pretty big day as well.'

They had told James about the horrific accident outside the hospital and how they'd worked together at the scene. Emma had wondered if the topic of conversation had been of such interest to James due to professional reasons or because it was a relief to stop talking or even thinking about the three young children under his roof. He was looking so tired now that it was clear he was struggling with the changes in his life as much, if not more than his son and Emma's heart went out to him. It was no surprise that he needed some time on his own and refused the offer of a drink or further company.

Max was silent until he'd put a glass of wine into Emma's hand and then poured himself a small glass of whisky in the drawing room.

'It's this tree,' he told her. 'I can understand why it's upsetting Dad so much. We haven't had a Christmas tree in this house since Mum died.'

'It can't be easy,' Emma agreed quietly. 'But it's important, isn't it? For the children. And...' She stepped closer to the sparsely decorated tree to touch one of the crooked stars, looking up at the angel/fairy who was listing badly to one side at the top. 'And it's a beautiful tree.'

Max sounded as if he was suppressing a snort of laughter as he put his glass down and reached up to straighten the angel.

'It's a bit sad compared to what I remember our Christmas trees being like. Mum was a true fan. She loved fairy lights and candles and had so many boxes of decorations her trees were works of art. It was always a special evening when Andy and I were allowed to help decorate the tree.'

'I think Ben will remember making that star and tying it onto this tree. His first Christmas with the new part of his family.'

Max was silent for a moment and then cleared his throat as if he was intending to change the subject. 'The last time I remember seeing you was at Christmas time,' he said, as if an amusing memory had just surfaced. 'Must be ten years ago? It was at that party...'

Oh...*help*...

Emma could feel spots of bright colour appear on her cheeks and she couldn't meet his glance. He *did* remember their kiss. For a heartbeat, she couldn't think of anything else. The distance of time had vanished and it might have been only seconds since he'd lifted his lips from hers. That tingle was back, dancing through her body before settling into a tight, hot knot somewhere deep in her gut. To try and cool it down Emma made herself remember what had happened next. That Max had laughed that kiss off as meaning nothing at all and she had followed his example a heartbeat later.

Max's tone was a little more hesitant when he broke the silence again. 'Do you know why I kissed you that night, Emma?'

It was her turn to suppress a sound of laughter. She turned away, heading for one end of the couch. 'You were carrying mistletoe,' she reminded him. 'You were kissing every woman at the party.'

'But you were the first. You were the reason I picked up that silly plastic mistletoe so I had an excuse.' He had picked up his glass again. 'Have you got any idea why I might have wanted to do that?'

Emma sat down on the soft leather cushion.

Did she want to know?

No. She didn't want to know that Max might have been as attracted to her as she had been to him. Because that might put a match to any residual attraction that might be there and…and something might happen…

Which actually meant—if she was really honest with herself—the answer to her silent question was yes. In fact, Emma wanted to know so badly she lifted her gaze when Max remained silent for a long moment, her eyebrows raised to encourage him to tell her.

'Tell me,' she said.

'I saw you crying.'

Shocked, Emma remained silent as Max came to sit down in his father's chair, between her end of the couch and the odd-looking Christmas tree.

'You didn't see me,' he continued quietly. 'And I wanted to try and make you smile again because I knew why you had been crying.'

Emma swallowed hard. 'Did you?'

'It was the day that little boy died. I've forgotten his name. The one who had such a severe case of hypoplastic left ventricle syndrome that the only way to save him would have been a heart transplant. We had just put a PICC line in a few days earlier to give him medication for his heart failure but it hadn't been enough and you'd been there when he—'

'Tyler,' Emma interrupted. 'His name was Tyler.'

'He was special to you.'

More than special. Emma had been totally in love with that ten-month-old baby who had a smile that lit up the room, despite how sick he was.

'He changed my life,' she whispered. 'More than you would believe.'

Max was giving her that look again. The one that made her feel as if he was seeing her properly for the first time. The one that made her feel as if she was the only person in the world that mattered at this very moment in time.

'I knew something big had changed the moment I saw you again in the Royal.' Max hadn't even blinked as he held her gaze. 'It took a while to recognise you. But what did it have to do with Tyler?'

Emma took a sip of her wine. And then another. This wasn't something she talked about. Or even thought about very much if she could help it. It was well in the past now and she was moving on as best she could. But Max's life had just changed as monumentally as Emma's had all those years ago and that gave them a new connection. That fragile new trust was still there as well, and trust always deserved a chance to be nurtured. She would be trusting him with an important part of her own heart if she did tell him her story but there was something in those astonishingly blue eyes that made her feel safe. That said she mattered enough to make her story important. Vital, even…

'I got pregnant,' she admitted. 'A few years after we worked together on that paediatric rotation.'

That didn't seem to surprise Max. 'We all knew you were destined for motherhood,' he said. 'You just loved being with those babies on the paediatric ward so much. Did you get married, then?'

'No. But I was with the person I believed I was going to marry. A paediatric surgeon called Richard. The pregnancy killed our relationship completely.'

'He didn't want children?'

'Oh, he wanted children. That baby wasn't going to be one of them, though. It became obvious during my second trimester scan that she wasn't going to survive. She was anencephalic.'

'Oh, my God...' Max drained his glass. 'I'm so sorry. That must have been so hard to have had to choose a termination at a late stage like that.'

'But I didn't.' Emma's voice was little more than a whisper. 'That was the problem. Richard wanted to get rid of the problem as fast as possible but I chose to carry my baby until she was due to be born. Because of Tyler.'

The pain was still there, wasn't it? The sense of betrayal. That someone who'd said they loved her wasn't prepared to support her in a challenge that was always going to be heartbreaking but felt important enough to be something she had to do in order to be true to herself.

Max was still staring at her so she could see the moment that comprehension dawned. His jaw visibly dropped. 'You carried a baby that you knew could never survive so that she could be a donor for babies like Tyler?'

Emma nodded, blinking hard to make sure she didn't let any tears escape. 'I thought I knew what I was doing. That it wouldn't be as hard as it turned out to be. Losing my relationship because of my choice made it harder, but, in a way, that was probably a good thing because it became obvious that we were too different to ever be happy together.' Emma drew in a shaky breath. 'What broke my heart even more was that she was born on Christmas Day. She only lived for a few hours.' Emma had to swipe away a tear that she hadn't fought off. 'I called her Holly.'

Max said nothing. He got up and went to the sideboard to pour himself another drink from the cut glass decanter. He stood there looking down at the amber liquid as he swirled it in his glass for a long time before he looked up at Emma. It was a look that went straight to her heart and she could feel its intensity in every cell of her body. This wasn't sexual in any way. It was respect. Admiration. Something that felt as if it was wrapping the threads of the connection they already had in a material that was strong enough to be impermeable.

'You're amazing, Em,' he told her. 'You know that, don't you?'

Emma shrugged off what seemed to be an over-the-top compliment, even if it was one that made her feel truly proud of the choice she had made. 'If I hadn't known Tyler maybe I would have made different choices. I might still be a paediatrician instead of a locum. I might be married to Richard and have had three more children and be spending my Christmases in Italy so that they could play with all their cousins…'

But Max was shaking his head. 'I'm glad you didn't,' he said. 'If this Richard couldn't support your choice to do such an incredibly brave and selfless thing then he wasn't someone you would have wanted to spend the rest of your life with, believe me.'

Emma blinked. He thought she was brave? Selfless? Amazing, even…? Would *he* have supported that choice? She had the feeling that he would have and that sparked something that was even more powerful than any physical attraction she was aware of for Max Cunningham. Stronger than friendship, in fact. You could fall in love with a man who could support you to do the really difficult things in life.

More than a little shocked by the thought, Emma had to break any eye contact with Max. Fortunately, she had an excuse to move because she'd just noticed that the bow in the string of the star Ben had tried so hard to attach to the tree had come undone and the star was on the floor. She stooped to pick it up and reattach it.

'I can't imagine how hard that Christmas Day must have been for you,' Max said, moments later. 'I'm really sorry you had to go through that alone.'

His voice was unexpectedly close as Emma

straightened up from tying the string, so she wasn't really surprised to find that Max had moved to come and stand beside her. Her body seemed to be startled, however, because it was waking up with an acute awareness of his proximity that was so powerful it was actually painful. More like a stabbing sensation than any pleasant tingle.

'I knew it was coming. I knew I'd be able to cope even though it was hard. And…there was a kind of joy to be found there, as well, knowing that other babies were going to get to go home because of what Holly could give them. One like Tyler, even, who got a heart that was going to work. And, later, I heard that her kidneys had been used…and her liver…'

Emma's voice trailed away. It was still such a bittersweet balance to think about, let alone say aloud. She cleared her throat. 'You've had Christmas Days that were just as tough,' she added. 'Losing your brother last year. Losing your mum when you were so young. That must have cast a shadow over every Christmas since then.'

'We just didn't do Christmas,' Max agreed. 'And that's why this is so hard for my dad.'

It wasn't just hard for James, though. This was just as hard for Max. A part of him had to be missing his mother all over again as he watched Ben and Tilly and Alice struggle to adapt to their new family. And was this year the first he'd ever put up a Christmas tree? Given the way he'd dismissed the whole seasonal celebration as 'commercial hype', she suspected that he had always avoided anything to do with trees or decorations. She also suspected that his avoidance had far more to do with grief than anything else. It gave them another connection but it felt different to her own experience of grief. Max's had started so long ago, when he was no more than a boy and, looking at it from the point of view of an outsider, Emma could see how sad it was. That a father and his sons had been so lost and there clearly hadn't been anyone to help them through their grief. They probably believed they could never change how they felt about Christmas, but how sad would it be if their aversion to celebrating was transferred to yet another generation?

Emma wished there was something she could do to help because this was a lot bigger than her own sadness that was associated with Christmas. This was all to do with three innocent children.

'Do you think he can cope?' she asked. She was referring to James but she held Max's gaze in the hope that he would realise she was asking about his own ability to manage an emotionally difficult situation.

'He'll have to,' Max said—and he could have been speaking for both his father and himself. 'The children are here to stay and... well...it would appear that there are rules when it comes to Christmas.'

Emma smiled. 'There are rules,' she said. 'And I expect Ben knows them all.'

Max was smiling back at her. A small smile that grew. And then grew a bit more.

'What?' she asked. 'What's funny?'

'Nothing,' Max said. 'I'm just pleased to see you smile. The last time I wanted to make that happen for you I had to kiss you.'

Emma could feel her own smile fading. The mention of that kiss again made the intense subject of their recent conversation start to fade instantly into the background and then it hung in the air between them.

Like a suggestion. As if they were both wondering what it would be like to do it again. As if they were both realising that perhaps they really *wanted* to do it again. They were standing so close together it wouldn't take much for one of them to move and if they held this eye contact any longer, that was what was going to happen. One of them would move and then Max would bend his head or Emma would stand on her tiptoes and they wouldn't need any mistletoe because they didn't need any reason to kiss other than that they were two single adults who happened to be attracted to each other. Possibly seriously attracted...

In that split second of time, however, as the ghost of their first kiss pulled them together like the most powerful magnet imaginable, a sound broke the moment. A crackle of sound that was coming from the handset of the baby monitor as Alice woke and began to cry.

'I'd better go and get her.' But Max seemed reluctant to move.

Emma opened her mouth to offer to help but no words came out because her thoughts were moving so fast they were getting tangled. Warning bells were ringing very loudly as she remembered the moment earlier this evening when that old longing for her own family had resurfaced. She couldn't afford— and didn't want—to get any closer to these children herself than she already was. And what about that moment when she'd realised how easy it would be to fall in love with Max? That should be enough to send her running all on its own because what she remembered most about this man was that he was a playboy. He'd never had the slightest interest in a relationship that was anything more than fun. Short term fun.

But it wasn't just the three bereaved children upstairs that Emma was thinking about right now. It was the two small boys who had lost their own mother decades ago and whose father must have been too wrapped up in his own grief to be able to know what to do and the end result was that they didn't know how to 'do Christmas' any more. Somehow, they needed to get past the ghosts of past Christmas tragedies, but that might not be possible without help from someone who hadn't been a part of that past.

Someone like Emma, who could understand how difficult it was but could also see how important it was for the sake of the children. She could do that if she was brave enough. The safe thing to do would be to remove herself from this house—to stay away from any more reminders of what was missing from her own life and away from the increasing pull she was feeling towards Max, but if she didn't run away—if she stayed here and helped both the Cunningham men and the children—it could be the foundation for a new family to form and bond. For a new life to be possible.

That would be a real gift, wouldn't it?

Not totally dissimilar to the choice she'd made more than five years ago, to do something hard in order to make new life possible for others. Max thought she was amazing for doing that.

Maybe she wanted him to think she was still amazing?

Emma took a deep breath. 'You go and get Alice,' she told Max. 'I'll get a bottle ready for you but then I really need to have a shower and get some sleep. I've got another early start tomorrow.'

Max still hadn't quite moved. 'And tomorrow?' he asked quietly. 'Will you come back here after work and help us put some more decorations on our tree?'

Oh…the warmth in those eyes. A mix of the new trust between them that had grown considerably this evening, shared memories of the past and the remnants of a kiss that hadn't quite happened. And behind what was there between herself and Max, Emma was aware of the needs of others. Of three children who badly needed something special to make them feel safe. Of a sad older man who was still suffering because his memories of Christmas were too painful. What James needed, as well as Max, was to be able to trust in family enough to open their hearts again. Emma could understand exactly why they had shut themselves off but she could also see how much better life would be if they could let go of the past and embrace a new future. And, if she could help them do that, she would be helping herself at the same time. She hadn't actually celebrated Christmas in any meaningful way herself since the day Holly had been born and died.

Maybe fate had brought her here because it was time for a new start. For all of them. It hadn't really been a mistake to come back here today. The mistake would be to leave before they had all taken that new step forwards.

Emma didn't trust herself to say anything aloud, though. All she could manage was to nod before she headed for the kitchen to make up the bottle of formula for Alice, but it was a definitive answer to Max's question nonetheless.

She would be here again tomorrow. And the next day.

And Christmas Day.

* * *

This was definitely getting a little easier.

Yesterday, in this very room, Max had been trying to feed a baby who wanted nothing to do with him. Now, he was sitting in his father's favourite chair, holding a baby who was almost asleep again before she'd got halfway through her bottle of milk. He should probably take her back upstairs and put her in her cot but he didn't want to move again just yet.

The shape of Alice in his arms was already becoming familiar. The smell of her, as well, as Max bowed his head to get closer to that small head cradled in the crook of his elbow. Imagine holding a baby like this, he thought—your own baby that you'd just given birth to—knowing that, in a blink of time, she would be taken away from you for ever. Max had been totally blown away by hearing Emma's story and his respect for her had gone completely off the scale. He'd never met a woman like her. He'd never met *anyone* like Emma Moretti, in fact.

He could understand now that it really had been fear he'd seen in her eyes the other night when Emma had come into the room to see him holding a miserable, hungry baby that he couldn't cope with. And what had he done? Simply shoved Alice into her arms, that was what, and he felt awful about that now. He wanted to gather Emma into his arms and tell her how sorry he was. Not just for forcing her to take Alice but for everything that had happened to her in the years since they'd gone on separate paths. For the grief she must have gone through. For the broken relationship, although he was quite confident that that Richard had not been good enough for Emma.

She was someone incredibly special. Astonishingly attractive, for that matter. He'd almost *kissed* her again, for heaven's sake. How had that happened in the wake of listening to her tragic story? And why had he longed to do it even more than the first time when all he'd wanted to do was to see that gorgeous smile appear again?

The reminder of that Christmas party made Max wonder if dealing with the aftermath of the grief of losing her baby Holly had contributed to her walking away from the career she had chosen because she loved children and babies so much? She was clearly very good at her locum work, fitting in instantly to new environments and being able to function brilliantly, but it didn't feel like the right fit for someone like Emma. In some ways, she reminded Max of his own mother—someone so clever and capable, with so much love to give the people lucky enough to be within her immediate circle.

It was weird that, even after decades, it was possible to feel a beat of that loss all over again, but it was muted enough that Max could easily refocus his thoughts. Emma was flitting from one job to another now, avoiding commitment to anything. To anyone? Did Christmas Day bring her any joy or was it only filled with unbearably sad memories?

He could understand that.

But…she'd said she was going to come back after work tomorrow and help with some more decorations. That she would stay until Christmas day, in fact. What if…?

Max gently removed the teat from Alice's now slack little rosebud of a mouth but he paused for a long moment before putting the bottle on the table beside him.

What if he could somehow make this Christmas something joyous for Emma? A time when she could smile and enjoy being with children and babies—a family, even? That might help her to take a step forward into a future that she really deserved, where grief could be outweighed by joy. Where sadness could be dimmed by the kind of light that laughter and love could create.

It wouldn't just help Emma. How good would it be for his father? For himself, perhaps, as well. It might not be easy but look at the way he and Emma had worked together today. If he could get her on board, by making it all about the children—or perhaps his father—they could help each other get past any personal issues. He could bury his distaste for the commercial hype of the season and hopefully Emma would get a glimpse of a future where she could see herself celebrating the family bonds that she believed Christmas was all about. A future that she could embrace with no restrictions or fear.

Not being at work meant that Max would have plenty of time to remember the way his mother had made the house come alive at Christmas time. He could go shopping—online, if necessary—to find gifts he could wrap up to go under the tree. He could ask Maggie to do a bit of Christmas baking so that the house would be filled with those delicious aromas he had a faint memory of. He could go up into the dusty attics of this house and drag out those dozens of boxes that contained miles of fairy lights and candles and every kind of decoration you could imagine.

Max looked down at the baby in his arms. He touched her cheek with his forefinger with the softest stroke.

'That's what I'm going to do,' he told Alice. 'For your big brother and sister. For my dad. For Emma. And don't worry, we'll take lots of photos so that it won't matter that you're not old enough to remember your first Christmas and it might be a good thing. This will be kind of a practice run and we'll be really good at it by the time you are old enough to remember.'

He got slowly to his feet, so as not to wake Alice, and carried her upstairs to her cot. It felt good that she was comforted enough to sleep again. It felt good to pass the door of the room not so far from his where he knew Emma would be tucked up in her bed and possibly also asleep.

And it felt really good that he had a mission for the next few days that might help Emma. And his father. Max had always worked hard and played hard. This mission was neither work nor play but the effort he was going to put into it was going to be a hundred and one per cent.

Because it mattered to everybody in this house and Max wanted to protect them all and give them the gift of joy. It might be focused only on one special day for now but it was a beginning and he was determined to make it the best one possible. For everyone, including Emma.

Maybe—given what he'd learned about her today—*especially* for Emma.

CHAPTER SEVEN

LOOPING HER STETHOSCOPE around her neck as she walked into the emergency department of the Royal early the next morning, Emma's steps slowed and almost stopped. Okay, it was Christmas Eve tomorrow, but what the heck were so many people doing in here wearing Santa suits? There had to be about ten of them—a sea of red and white in the cubicle area for injured or ill patients that weren't serious enough to need to be in one of the resuscitation rooms.

Senior nurse Miriam was trying to keep a straight face. 'Seems like it was rather a good Christmas party,' she told Emma. 'There were too many people dancing on the table and a leg broke.'

Emma's eyebrows rose. 'A table leg or a person's leg?'

Miriam's smile escaped. 'The table, but there is a guy with an ankle injury, a woman with a possibly fractured wrist and quite a few bumps and bruises. The others are their partners or colleagues so we couldn't tell them to go away.'

'Who needs to be seen first?'

'Ankle Santa, I think. He's the boss. He's also rather drunk so he might be injured more than he realises.'

The middle-aged man was still wearing his red hat with white fur trim. Having glanced at the chart on the end of his bed that told her his vital signs were all within normal limits, Emma introduced herself and then asked how he was feeling.

'Never better,' he told her. 'It was the best party ever. Gonna need a new table in the boardroom, though.'

Several Santas, including one that called from the next cubicle, seemed to be in agreement that it had been a memorable party.

'It must have been good,' Emma agreed, 'if it went on till nearly dawn.'

'Oh, I don't think it's finished yet.' A

woman wearing a red dress with white trim-
ming and a headband with a small red hat
in the middle was holding her arm cradled
against her chest, which suggested she was
the patient with the wrist injury. 'There was
a new case of prosecco being opened when
our taxis arrived to bring us here.'

'Hmm...' Emma was already assessing the
ankle injury of the man lying on the bed. It
was certainly swollen enough to be either a
serious sprain or a fracture but his toes were
a good colour and she could feel a peripheral
pulse on the top of the foot. 'Can you try and
wriggle your toes for me, please?'

She watched the movement and heard the
groan that told her it was causing pain but
Emma was not quite as focused as she would
normally have been. It wasn't just being surrounded by an unusual number of people
dressed like Father Christmas who were all
inebriated to some extent. It was more the
mention of the Italian bubbly they'd been
drinking, in combination with knowing that
it had been a Christmas party. Because it im-

ALISON ROBERTS

191

mediately made her think of *that* particular party. That particular kiss.

The kiss that had very nearly happened again last night.

How much she had wanted it to happen had been the reason she'd left Max to cope alone with feeding Alice and why she'd slipped out of the house early this morning before anyone else was up. Things were complicated enough in the Cunningham household without letting a sexual attraction get out of hand. Emma wanted to help weld the new family of James, Max and the children together but, at some point in her almost sleepless night, she had decided that even the casual type of relationship that Max Cunningham was famous for would only be a distraction from what he needed to be focused on—the children—so her mission needed to be to keep him on task. If that wasn't exactly what she wanted, she was prepared to deal with it for the sake of everybody else involved.

She needed to keep herself on task as well.

'Have you ever injured this ankle before?'

'Nope. Mind you, I've never done the floss dance before, either.'

'You were really good at it.' A much younger Santa poked his head around the curtain. 'I'm still trying to figure it out.' He straightened his arms and held them out, staring at them as if he was trying to decide which one to move.

'Move your hips first,' someone called. 'Get the rhythm.'

'Uh-uh...' The firm voice belonged to Miriam. 'No dancing in here, folks. If you're well enough to dance, you need to go out to the waiting room. We've got sick people in here.' She tilted her head in Emma's direction. 'You need any help, Dr Moretti?'

Emma shook her head. 'But call me if anything major comes in.'

'I'm major,' her patient told her. 'Don't leave me, darlin'.'

'Do you have any medical conditions I should be aware of? Heart disease or high blood pressure? Diabetes or lung problems?'

'Nah. I'm as fit as a fiddle. Or I will be. I've asked Santa for a gym subscription this year. In fact, I think I asked several Santas.'

A ripple of laughter came from adjoining cubicles. 'Wasn't me,' someone called.

'I don't remember being asked,' someone else shouted. 'But I can't remember much at all right now, come to think of it.'

Emma was examining the ankle more closely. She put her hand under the foot near the toes. 'Can you push your foot against my hand, please?' She shifted her hand to the top of the foot next. 'Pull up against it, now?'

'Ouch.'

'I don't think it's broken,' Emma told him a short time later. 'But we'll send you off for an X-ray just to be on the safe side.'

The woman with the wrist injury was also sent to X-ray, but the other injuries were deemed minor and the crowd of red and white patients gradually dispersed, some beginning to complain of headaches and feeling rather unwell.

'Christmas parties,' Miriam muttered, shaking her head. 'More trouble than they're worth most of the time.'

'Mmm.' Emma needed to stop thinking about Christmas parties.

About Max and being thoroughly kissed by him.

Her next patient, coming in by ambulance already intubated and being ventilated after what appeared to be a serious stroke, was more than enough to give Emma complete focus on her job and that continued for the rest of her shift, with one case after another that required rapid assessment and treatment to stabilise them. There was an elderly man with septic shock, a drug overdose, pulmonary embolism, two heart attacks and a ten-year-old child with a severe asthma attack who needed transferring to the intensive care unit for close monitoring when she was finally out of immediate danger.

Emma was still thinking about that last case as she drove back to Upper Barnsley. The child's mother had burst into tears when told that the worst seemed to be over.

'She'd just been writing a reminder list for Father Christmas,' she sobbed. 'And I was feeling so smug because I've already got everything hidden away but...but I've just had an hour to wonder what it would have been like if they'd never been unwrapped...'

Those gifts would get unwrapped and that made it a good note on which to have finished her day. It had also reminded Emma that Max had asked her to find out what Ben and Tilly might have asked to receive for a special Christmas gift. Maybe when she got home she could help them write a list to put up the chimney. She was all ready to suggest this to Max the minute she walked through the door, but she didn't get a chance to say anything.

'Come with me.' It looked as if he'd been waiting for her to get home. 'We haven't got long.'

He grabbed Emma by the hand and started to head upstairs. Towards the bedrooms? Emma thought about tugging her hand free and trying to find out what was going on, but the warmth of Max's hand around hers and the determination of his forward movement was irresistible and all Emma could actually think about was that she'd probably go anywhere with this man if he wanted her to—

even to a totally unknown destination. It was exciting. Thrilling, even. Especially the feeling of his skin against hers as they hurried upstairs. Her resolution to stay away from any intimate involvement with him seemed to be fading rapidly as the heat and feeling of strength in the hand holding hers made her curl her fingers tighter to make sure the connection wouldn't be lost.

They went past the bedrooms, into another hallway Emma hadn't seen before, with old portraits hanging on the walls, and then up a smaller staircase.

'The servants' quarters were up here long before my family moved in,' Max told her. 'It's where we used to hide when we were kids, Andy and me.'

'Is that what we're doing? Playing hide and seek with Ben and Tilly?'

'No.' They were up the small staircase now and leaving footprints on dust-covered floorboards. 'They're in the kitchen with Maggie and her daughter Ruth. Ruth's just gone on maternity leave from her job as an infant school teacher and she's brilliant with the kids. They're icing Christmas cookies at the moment. Alice is asleep. Dad's out on a house call. It's the first chance I've had all day to do this.' He stopped to peer up yet another staircase that was steep and narrow enough to be more like a ladder. Then he grinned at Emma. 'The main attic's up here,' he added, letting go of her hand as he started to climb. 'And there should be enough Christmas decorations to sink a battleship, if they haven't been eaten by mice or something. I need some help getting them downstairs but I didn't want Ben trying to get up and down these stairs. And I didn't want Dad to know what I was doing because he would have tried to stop me. He won't like it but if we can start putting them up I figured he would see how much fun it is for the kids and…and…'

'He won't want to disappoint them.' Emma nodded as she followed Max up the narrow stairs. 'A bit of emotional blackmail, huh? Well, it certainly worked on me.'

'What? When?' Max sounded appalled.

'When you reminded me about telling the

children I'd show them how to make stars. Or getting them to remind me...'

'Oh...' Max disappeared through the hole in the ceiling and then turned to offer his hand to help Emma as she reached the final stairs. Having been holding it so recently, it felt completely natural to take it again, allowing him to pull her into the attic space. He was still smiling as he tugged her forward.

'Do you forgive me?' he asked. 'For emotionally blackmailing you?'

'It was for a good cause.' Emma realised that if she kept that forward momentum going she would end up bumping into Max's body. He'd probably put his hands on her shoulders to steady her and it might very well be an opportunity to pick up where they'd left off last night. To step back into that 'pre-kiss' moment if she wanted to.

She did want to. Very much. But, at the same time, it was making her nervous. Emma put the brakes on that forward movement unconsciously and, for a heartbeat, she stood completely still. She was now aware of the faint light coming from dormer windows in this highest level of the house. It was crowded with boxes and furniture and any amount of objects and it smelled musty and secretive. Even without kissing Max, it was still exciting because she'd never been in a real, storybook kind of attic before and they were here together and…and, well…

It was fun. And how long was it since Emma had done anything just for the sheer enjoyment of it?

'Look…there's one.' Max let go of Emma's hand to open a box. 'It's the fake greenery,' he exclaimed, moments later. 'I remember that Mum used to wind it through the bannister posts on the main stairs. And this one…' He pulled open another box. 'It's fairy lights. We need fairy lights on our tree, don't we?'

'Absolutely.' Emma was reaching for another box on the stack. This one was full of objects wrapped in tissue paper. 'Decorations,' she exclaimed. 'Oh, look…it's fruit. Little silver and gold apples and pears. And red cherries.'

'Don't open them yet.' Max caught her hand

as she delved further into the box. 'Let's take them downstairs and the kids can help us.'

The touch of his hand, yet again, was more than enough to stop Emma. Turning her head, she found she was just as close to Max as they'd been last night beside the Christmas tree when she had been sure they would have ended up kissing if Alice's cry hadn't interrupted the moment. There was no baby's cry happening right now and they were possibly in the most secret part of this huge old house but, as Emma's gaze locked with Max's, she knew that they weren't about to steal a kiss. It felt as if they were making a kind of silent pact in this moment. That this was about the children and they were equal partners on the same team. Which was pretty much the conclusion Emma had reached last night, however tempting it might be to explore this unexpected revival of a seemingly mutual attraction between herself and Max. And it would appear that Max had decided the same thing.

She shouldn't be disappointed, Emma told herself firmly. She wasn't. Not really...

If she told herself that often enough, maybe she would actually believe it.

Oh, man…

He wanted to kiss Emma so much. Had she noticed that he couldn't seem to stop himself touching her? She'd been perfectly capable of climbing those stairs or getting up into the attic all by herself and here he was, holding her hand again, under the pretext of stopping her unwrapping any more decorations.

And the way she was looking at him. As if she wanted him to kiss her?

Well, he couldn't and that was all there was to it. Giving in to the temptation was the way the old Max would have responded. The one who was happy to play with any number of beautiful women. To love them and leave them and give himself a reputation that he was, finally, rather ashamed of. He had far more important responsibilities now and, besides, he respected Emma far too much to think that she might be happy to indulge in a casual affair.

She seemed perfectly happy to play Christmas decorations with him, however. Together, they ferried box after box downstairs and, as Max had been hoping, Ben and Tilly were so excited about what was inside all the boxes that they were almost unrecognisable compared to the silent, scared children who'd been sitting on the couch in the drawing room only a few evenings ago.

Maggie and her pregnant daughter Ruth were staying on to help—as curious as the children about what was being unearthed from decades of storage. Alice lay, still sleeping, in her pram near the couch as they spread out the boxes and opened them all.

'Look at these cute bunches of bells.' Ruth held up a trio of tiny golden bells, tied together with a loop of red ribbon.

'They went on the doors,' Max told her. 'So they would jingle every time someone went in or out of a room. And that really big wreath? That's for the front door.'

'There are so many candles.' Maggie had opened another box. 'And what's this? A tablecloth? And Christmas serviettes?'

'I don't think we'll need them,' Max said.

'I'm not sure I'd know where to start making a Christmas dinner.'

Maggie and her daughter shared a glance. 'Perhaps we could help,' she said. 'It was only going to be me and Ruth at our house and we've got a turkey that's far too big for just the two of us. We could come here and do dinner for everybody if you like.'

'What do you think, Ben?' Max asked. 'Are there rules about Christmas dinner?'

Ben nodded. 'Pigs in blankets,' he said. 'And red jelly for pudding.'

Maggie laughed. 'I think we could manage that.' She looked at Emma. 'You'll be here for dinner, I hope?'

'It sounds great,' Emma said. 'I'm covering a night shift on Christmas Eve so I'll definitely be back in time for dinner.'

Max wound a long string of fairy lights all over the tree in the drawing room but told Ben and Tilly to stand back while he plugged them in and turned the switch on. 'I'm not quite sure what's going to happen,' he told them. 'These lights haven't been used for a very long time.'

'Why not?' Ben asked.

'Because they were my mum's—your grandma's—special Christmas things and… well, she died and we were very sad so we never used them again.'

'Why not?' Ben was frowning. 'You've got to have lights on your Christmas tree. It's a—'

'—rule. I know.' Max flicked the switch and the lights came to life, making the tree sparkle as they flashed on and off sequentially. Instead of having bulbs that didn't work any more, or wires that caught fire because they had deteriorated over the years, it looked as if these decorative lights were as good as new. Max decided he was going to take that as a good omen. That everything was going to work and sparkle with a bit of Christmas magic.

'My mummy's died too.' Tilly's bottom lip was wobbling. 'And *I'm* sad.'

'I know, sweetheart.' From the corner of his eye, Max saw Emma start to reach out to Tilly but then he saw the way she stopped herself—the way her hands curled into soft fists—as if she was just too afraid to let herself follow her natural instinct to comfort this small girl. So he was the one who went to Tilly to scoop her up and cuddle her. He resisted the urge to draw Emma into the hug as well. If he tried to force her to open her heart to these children she might change her mind about staying to share Christmas with them and run away. He could only hope that some of that sparkly Christmas magic would wrap itself around Emma and she could find the courage to step past the perfectly understandable fear she had and that, by doing so, she would see what a new future could offer her.

'Can you help me?' he asked Tilly. 'You could unwrap all the ornaments in that box and then we can all hang them on the tree.'

'There's this green stuff too,' Emma said, pulling at loops of the long, thin length of artificial foliage of ivy, mistletoe and holly with red berries. 'I could go and put that on the bannisters, perhaps? And hang the bells on the doors?'

If it was time away from the children that she needed, it wasn't going to work. Ben's eyes widened as he saw the impressive amount of greenery appearing.

'I want to help,' he said.

'Me too.' Tilly wriggled out of Max's arms. 'I like bells *and* stars.'

She was almost running in her haste to get closer to Emma when it happened. The door-frame of the drawing room was filled with the tall figure of James Cunningham and the furious vibe radiated from him with the speed of light.

'What the *hell* is going on here?' he roared. 'Where did you get those boxes?'

'From the attic, Dad.' Max kept his tone carefully neutral. 'We needed more decorations for the tree.'

But his words could barely be heard over the sound of children crying. The angry roar had made Ben cower behind Emma's legs, still holding one end of a garland of greenery. Tilly had burst into tears and even Alice had woken in her pram and started howling. Maggie and Ruth both moved towards the baby. He saw the way Emma instinctively stretched out her arms as if creating a safe circle for the two children close to her. She was glaring at his father, as well, looking both horrified and angry that he was scaring everybody.

Max was angry too, even though part of his heart was breaking for his dad. He'd known his father would be upset at having his wife's precious decorations appear again with no prior warning but it wasn't fair to take it out on the children like this. Even Pirate was looking worried, slinking away from James to hide beneath one of the chairs.

'You've got no right.' James's voice was still loud enough to qualify as shouting. 'Put them back. Ben...put that down. Right now.'

The garland slid instantly from Ben's hands.

Max cleared his throat. 'If Mum was here, this is exactly what she'd be doing,' he told his father.

'I want *my* mummy,' Tilly sobbed, sinking into a puddle of miserable child on the floor. Ben came out from behind Emma and crouched to put his arms around his little sister. Pirate came out from beneath the chair and went slowly towards the children. He sat down close to Tilly and pressed his nose to the hands covering her eyes. Perhaps it was the surprise of seeing the little dog as she opened her eyes that made her stop crying.

Maggie was rocking baby Alice and successfully soothing her. Ruth had her hands protectively on the impressive bump of her belly and was staring nervously at her mother's employer. Max shifted his gaze to Emma to find she was staring straight back at him. If he'd had any doubts at all about her level of commitment to help him make this Christmas special for the children, they evaporated instantly. In the face of opposition she had just become as determined as he was to make this work. She was going to do whatever it took to protect these children, even if she had to do it alone, but she wanted his help. She needed him to be by her side and that made him feel remarkably fierce.

He would do whatever it took to protect Emma, as well as the children.

'It's what Mum would have wanted us to do, Dad,' he said firmly. 'You know that. You know how much she loved Christmas. How much she wanted everyone to be happy. I know it's been a very long time but we are going to have a proper Christmas in this house this year.'

James was staring at the boxes. At the huge wreath that Maggie had put to one side to take out to the front door. At the bunches of bells and the tissue-wrapped decorations.

'Oh…do what you want, then,' he snapped. 'You're obviously going to, anyway. I'm going out.' He snapped his fingers. 'Pirate…come with me…'

But Pirate didn't move. If anything, the little dog pressed itself closer to Tilly and Ben's hand moved to rest on the small white head. For a horrified moment, Max wondered if his father was about to march further into the room and drag his dog away from the children but James just stared for a moment longer, made a sound that was a frustrated growl and then turned on his heel and marched out of the room.

For a long, long moment, there was silence

in the drawing room. It was broken by Ben's small voice.

'I don't think Grandpa likes Christmas,' he said.

Max walked over to his nephew and crouched down beside him. 'He used to,' he told Ben. 'It was the best day of the year for all of us when I was a little boy like you. He's just forgotten, that's all. But we can help him remember. He's not cross with you. He's just...'

'Sad.' Ben nodded. 'Because his mummy died.'

Max didn't bother trying to correct his interpretation of a former generation's relationships. 'It's always sad when someone you love dies,' he agreed. 'And it's okay to be sad but it's okay to have fun too. Why don't we all have fun now and see how pretty we can make everything with all these decorations? Do you think you and Tilly can pull that long rope of leaves and berries all the way up the stairs?'

Max caught Emma's anxious glance as the children headed for the door.

'It's all right,' he said. 'Dad will have gone out for a walk or something. He just needs time to get his head around this.'

Emma didn't look convinced.

'It's been a very long time,' Max added. 'I suspect he's healed far more than he even realises but he's never going to find out if that plaster doesn't get ripped off. Having a proper Christmas with his grandchildren might be the best thing that could ever happen for him.'

Emma was still frowning. 'As long as he doesn't hurt the children. Don't you think Ben's going to be a bit scared of him after that outburst?'

'Maybe.' Max was holding Emma's gaze. 'But I think he's going to be fine. Even the scary stuff isn't too bad as long as you've got someone on your side and Ben's got me. He's always going to have me.'

Would Emma pick up on the silent message that he was there for her as well? That she had him by her side as she faced what was probably her first real celebration of Christmas for a long time?

Maybe she had. There was a sparkle in her

eyes that looked as if a tear or two was gathering.

'He's a lucky little boy,' she said quietly. 'And I think you're right. He's going to be fine.'

'He'll need help with that green stuff. Why don't I come and show you how Mum used to do it and then we can all do the decorations for the tree?'

It was much later that evening that Emma went down the stairs, admiring the greenery woven through the bannister railings, heading for the kitchen to get a glass of water. To her surprise, she found Max sitting at the kitchen table with his laptop open in front of him and the handset from the baby monitor to one side. James was also there, an empty plate in front of him that told Emma he'd eaten the meal they'd left in the oven when he hadn't come home in time for dinner.

'I owe you an apology too,' he said gruffly.

Emma nodded her acceptance. 'The children missed you at bedtime,' she told him. 'They wanted you to read them a story. Ben said that it might make you feel better because stories always make *him* feel better.'

James stared at her for a long moment. 'You always know the right thing to say, don't you, love? You're like my Hannah was, like that.' He got to his feet. 'I'm off to bed,' he said. 'But I'd better take Pirate out first. It's starting to snow and he doesn't like it when it gets too deep on the grass. Do you know where he is?'

'Lying beside Ben's bed,' Emma told him. 'I think he's decided it's his job to protect the children.'

'He's not the only one, is he?' James put his plate in the sink. 'It's okay… Now that I'm over the shock, I know I was wrong and I'll tell the children that tomorrow. It's time for Christmas to happen again here. Time for a new beginning.' He smiled at Emma. 'Maybe I should write my Christmas wish on a bit of paper too, and you could put it up the chimney. Max told me about you doing that for the children this evening.'

'It's what I'm working on now,' Max put in.

'Seeing if I can find exactly what they want online and get it delivered secretly tomorrow.'

'Didn't Ben say he wanted a blue bicycle?' Emma reminded him. 'That might be a bit hard to keep secret.'

'There's some rooms that aren't being used above the clinic. Extra bedrooms and a bathroom or two. It could make a good suite for live-in help for a housekeeper or nanny later, maybe. In the meantime, it'll be easy to get things delivered out of sight and hide them in there, wrap them up tomorrow night and put them under the tree for Christmas morning.'

James was heading for the door. 'Don't forget the stockings.' His voice was a growl. 'The ones your mum always hung up above the fireplace. They must be in one of those boxes.'

Max waited until his father had left the room. 'He's trying hard,' he said quietly. 'It's not easy.'

'I know. For you too.' Emma had been watching Max as they'd decorated the tree earlier. She'd seen the way he'd held some of those decorations so reverently—like the gorgeous glass angels and wooden gingerbread men—as if he was remembering the last time he'd done this, when his mother had been there as well, and her heart had ached for that little boy who must have dreaded Christmas for so many years afterwards.

She pulled up a chair to sit close beside him so that she could see the screen of his laptop. 'How are you going on finding things?'

'Not bad. Derby's has a great toy department. I've found a bicycle for Ben and a football and a tent.'

'A tent?'

'It was something that Andy and I used to do—put a tent up in the woods and pretend we were miles from anywhere. I thought Ben might like to try that.'

'It's a great idea.'

'I'm not sure what Tilly meant by "fairy stuff", though.'

'Oh... I can help with that.' Emma leaned closer so that she could use the mouse and scroll through the available items. 'Look... a tutu, wand, tiara and wings all in a set. There's even a pot of fairy dust, which is probably glitter and will make an awful mess. That's what "fairy stuff" is all about.'

Emma looked up, her smile full of the delight of imagining the look on Tilly's face when she discovered exactly what Emma had helped her write on her scrap of paper that had gone up the chimney. She hadn't realised just how close she'd got to Max as she leaned over the laptop, however. And she hadn't expected him to be grinning down at her, as pleased as she was to have found the perfect gift.

And there it was.

That moment again, as their gazes locked and their smiles faded as they both found they couldn't look away from each other. That the magnetic pull was simply too powerful to resist.

'Thanks.' Max's voice was a little hoarse. A deep, sexy growl. 'I wouldn't be managing this if I didn't have you to help.'

'Oh…it's my pleasure.' Emma's voice was more like a whisper and her last word was the one that tipped the balance of control. *Pleasure…* It hung there between them and she knew that Max was thinking exactly the same as what was going through her own head. That real pleasure was also hanging there, just waiting for one of them to make the first move.

Maybe both of them did, because a split second later their lips were touching. So softly at first that Emma had to close her eyes so that she could feel it properly. And then she felt the movement of Max's lips on hers and her own lips parting. The kiss wasn't so soft now but it was when she was aware of the touch of his tongue on her lip before meeting the tip of her own tongue that Emma stopped even thinking about what was happening and fell into a forgotten sensation.

Sheer pleasure, that was for sure. So intense that nothing else existed. This was nothing like that public kiss under the mistletoe at that long-ago Christmas party. This was nothing like any kiss Emma had ever had in her life. She didn't want it to stop but the need for oxygen made it a necessity and her first breath was a gasp. She opened her eyes to find Max staring at her, looking as stunned as she was feeling.

Oh…*help*…

This wasn't supposed to have happened.

Emma braced herself for what was about to happen next. Laughter, perhaps, to dismiss the kiss as no big deal? The reassurance that she had nothing to worry about because she was 'so not' Max's type?

As he opened his mouth to say something, Emma closed her eyes so that she could hide her reaction to whatever he might be about to say.

CHAPTER EIGHT

MAX HAD NO idea what to say but felt the need to express appreciation for what had to have been the most memorable kiss of his lifetime and that was saying something, given how much practice he'd had.

There was something very different about Emma Moretti. It wasn't just the softness of her lips, or the incredible taste of her mouth, or the way she responded to him as if they were having a conversation in a language they were the only two people in the world who could speak. It was bigger than that. Because he'd come to realise that Emma was the most extraordinary woman he'd ever met and he had huge respect for her, professionally but even more on a personal level.

That she had chosen to go through such a traumatic experience as carrying a baby for months that was never going to survive only to help others was something he felt put Emma way out of his league in terms of humanity and kindness and the kind of virtues that nobody would associate with someone who had his kind of reputation with women. It made him feel curiously shy to even think that she might be interested in him but that kiss had just revealed that she was possibly just as attracted to him as he was to her. That she might, in fact, be just as desperate to take it a lot further than just a kiss.

Just a kiss?

Ha! The words that finally escaped Max's lips were not ones he normally used in public but he needed something very succinct and powerful to sum up his reaction. His words certainly startled Emma. Her eyes flew open and then widened in shock.

'I thought you were going to laugh,' she said. 'Not say...*that*...'

'Why on earth would I laugh?'

'That's what you did the last time you kissed me.'

'Did I?' Max searched his memory. 'No...

I think it was *you* that laughed and I was pleased that you were looking happier again because that was what I wanted to happen.'

'You laughed first,' Emma insisted. 'And then you told me not to worry because I was so not your type.'

Oh…that was true. But not true at the same time. Even then he'd known precisely how attractive Emma Moretti was but she definitely wasn't his 'type' because she was dangerous. Or he was dangerous as far as she was concerned. She wanted such different things out of life and he would have ended up hurting her if he'd acted on that attraction. How ironic was it that he was the one who'd ended up with a bunch of kids and Emma was footloose and fancy free, roaming the world and perfectly entitled to work and play wherever and with whomever she chose.

Another thought that was a little disturbing was that if Emma had remembered his exact words after all this time, was it because he'd managed to hurt her anyway when he'd been trying to make sure he didn't? Max held Emma's gaze.

'No man in his right mind wouldn't have fancied you, Emma. I said that because I knew I wasn't *your* type. Maybe I wanted to say it before you did.'

'You weren't my type,' Emma agreed. There was a tiny smile tugging at one corner of her mouth. 'You were the "love 'em and leave 'em" bad boy of that group of registrars. But no woman in her right mind wouldn't have fancied you.'

Max found it suddenly rather difficult to swallow. Was she saying what he thought she might be saying? That she had fancied him? That she still did? He could find that out, he thought, if he kissed her again. If Emma wanted him to kiss her again. And, if she did, then he could scoop her up into his arms and take her…where…to his bedroom?

Where Alice lay sleeping in her cot?

His head turned to where the baby monitor handset was sitting beside his laptop. Emma had followed the direction of his gaze and he heard the sigh as she let her breath go. The reminder of the close proximity of three children was creating enough of a problem even theoretically. The small voice they both heard at the kitchen door a second later made it even more of a reality.

'Uncle Max?'

He turned swiftly. 'What is it, Ben?'

'I woke up.'

'I can see that, mate.' Max shut the lid of his laptop before Ben could see that he'd been surfing the toy department of Derby's. 'Did you have a bad dream?'

'Pirate's run away.'

'No, he hasn't.' Emma was smiling reassuringly at Ben. 'Your grandpa just took him outside for a little walk. He'll be back any minute.'

Her gaze snagged Max's and it was another reminder of how difficult it was going to be to find time to be alone in the near future, if ever. It wasn't as if Emma was even going to be here for very long, either. Was he crazy to think that getting to know this amazing woman on a more intimate level was possible, let alone a sensible idea? It felt like Emma was thinking along the same lines. It also felt like she was reaching the same conclusions.

That it was no more crazy than this set of totally unexpected circumstances they had found themselves in, temporarily living together in this old house with orphaned children, their grandfather and his dog and with a Christmas celebration to orchestrate when they'd both been avoiding doing something like that for many years. That they were both single adults and, if they wanted to, they could choose to indulge in a sexual attraction that wasn't going to hurt anybody else. And that the attraction between them wasn't about to vanish any time soon and perhaps they both needed to find out if it could live up to its promise of being one of those experiences that you might only find once in a lifetime.

Not that they were about to get the chance to find that out right now. Max needed to get Ben settled back into his bed but, as he led his nephew out of the kitchen, the front door of the house opened and his father and Pirate came inside. He felt Ben's hand clutch his fingers more tightly but the brave little boy straightened as he stood beside Max, as if he was getting ready to be growled at again by his grandfather.

Emma had come out of the kitchen as well so, for a moment, they all stood there holding their breath. It was Pirate who broke the tension, trotting towards Ben with his tail wagging. Ben let go of his uncle's hand and dropped to cuddle the small white dog.

'I think Pirate wants to go back to bed,' James said into the silence that followed. 'Shall I come and tuck you both in?'

This silence was even more tense and Max let his breath out in a silent but very relieved sigh as, after staring at his grandfather for a long moment, Ben nodded solemnly and started walking towards him. He had almost reached him when there was a loud thumping on the door behind James.

'What the—?' James opened the door. *Jenny...?*'

'Oh, Dr Cunningham—I'm so sorry to disturb you at this time of night but I saw you walking past. It's Terry. I think he really is having a heart attack this time...'

Both Max and Emma were moving towards

the distressed woman. Emma reached for her coat on the rack near the door. 'I'll come,' she told Jenny. 'Have you called an ambulance?'

'Yes, but it's really snowing hard now and I'm not sure if they'll get through.'

Max didn't bother finding his coat. 'I'll get our first-aid pack from the clinic,' he told Emma. 'And the defibrillator. I'll meet you there in a minute.'

He turned back to find that his father was holding Ben's hand. 'Don't worry,' he told Max. 'I've got this. You go with Emma. I'll look after the children.'

'You sure?'

'Yes. Take your phone. I'll call if I need you. Go…'

Max must have run very fast, both to collect the equipment and then get down the long driveway, up the road and into the neighbouring property so quickly. Emma had only had minutes to start assessing Terry.

'The pain came on about twenty minutes ago,' she told Max. 'Central chest pain, radiating to his left arm. Ten out of ten, with vomiting and profuse sweating. Unrelieved by his spray. Radial pulse palpable but faint.'

They were classic symptoms of a heart attack and nothing like the pain he had presented with after his muscle strain the other day. He also had other symptoms that made it far less likely to be anything muscular. Max opened pouches on the defibrillator pack and began unrolling wires and snapping electrodes onto their ends.

'There's an IV roll in the pack,' he told Emma. 'And a small oxygen tank in the side pocket.'

'Onto it.' Emma put a reassuring hand on Terry's shoulder. 'Max is going to do what I did the other day and put the electrodes on your chest so we can see what's going on with your heart. I'm going to give you some oxygen and put a small cannula in a vein on your arm so that we can give you something for the pain. We're going to give you some fluid through that line as well, to help your blood pressure. Is that all okay with you?'

Terry nodded. He was looking terrified. So was his wife.

'Do whatever you need to,' Jenny whispered. 'Please…'

Emma opened the IV roll and found everything she needed to put an IV line in. There was a separate pouch that contained drugs in both ampoules and packets. She popped a tablet from its foil strip.

'I'll get you to chew this up for me first,' she told Terry. 'It's an aspirin tablet. Jenny, maybe you could get a sip of water to help it go down?'

Jenny looked relieved to be given a helpful task. Emma focused on gaining access to a vein on the back of Terry's hand with a needle and then sliding the plastic cannula into place and taping it down securely. Max was working around her, sticking electrodes to Terry's shoulders and each side of his abdomen and then in a pattern across his chest and around his heart. They were working together, as smoothly as they had the day they had been treating the victims of that multi-car pile-up outside the Royal, but it felt different now. The professional trust they already had was coloured by a far more personal connection. Not that either of them would have been giving that kiss a moment's head space but it was there, somewhere in the background, and it had brought them a whole lot closer.

'Are you allergic to any medications?' Emma asked.

'No...' Terry's voice was slightly muffled behind the oxygen mask that was now in place.

'Is the pain still ten out of ten?'

Terry closed his eyes as he nodded. Jenny was hunched over the back of the chair her husband was slumped in, one hand pressed against her mouth, the other stroking Terry's head.

'I'm going to give you some morphine,' Emma told him. 'As well as something else to stop you feeling sick. You should notice a difference in the pain very soon.'

'And I need you to keep as still as possible, Terry,' Max said. 'I'm going to take a recording of your heart now.'

He looked up to catch Emma's gaze as the graph paper began to spill out of the monitor. He knew she had seen the big picture of what was going on already on the screen and that Terry was, indeed, having a heart attack.

'ST elevation leads two, three and aVF,' Max confirmed as he showed Emma the printout. 'T wave changes starting.'

'Inferior infarct,' Emma agreed quietly. Heart attacks in this region had a better prognosis than other regions but it was still time critical to get Terry to hospital for the definitive treatment that would reopen his coronary arteries.

'I'll ring the hospital,' Max offered. 'They can get the catheter lab team on standby for angioplasty.'

'Can you find out how far away the ambulance is?' Emma asked. 'And do they have transmission ability so we can send the twelve-lead ECG through first?'

Max nodded. 'Yes, and yes.'

Emma turned back to their patient. 'How's the pain now, Terry?'

'Better.'

'On the scale of zero to ten?'

'Maybe five.'

'That's great. I'm going to take your blood

pressure and a few other measurements now. Try and relax. We're going to get you to hospital very soon.'

'So he is really having a heart attack this time?'

'It looks like it, Jenny. But try not to worry too much, okay? The treatment of angioplasty will stop the damage that's happening. You did exactly the right thing in calling the ambulance and then coming to find us so quickly, which meant we could start the treatment faster.'

'Ambulance is only a few minutes away,' Max reported as Emma wrote down the set of vital signs she had just taken. 'Apparently the road's not too bad with the snow yet and the call's gone out to the cath lab. They're expecting Terry in Emergency as well.'

'Jenny? Could you go and pack a bag for Terry? Just his pyjamas and toothbrush and things he might need for a day or two in hospital?'

Again, Jenny seemed grateful for something useful she could do and she had accomplished her task by the time the paramedics arrived with a dusting of snow on their shoulders and a cheerful ambience that was immediately reassuring.

'How lucky are you to have doctors living next door?' they said to Terry. 'Looks like they've done all the hard work for us too. We just need to put you on our comfy stretcher, change you over to our monitor and oxygen and we'll be at the hospital in no time at all.'

'Can I come with him?' Jenny asked anxiously.

'Of course you can, love.'

'I can come as well.' Emma picked up her coat from where it had been thrown over the back of a couch.

'No need, Doc. You've done everything already and all we need to do is keep a close eye on Terry here until we get him into the Royal.'

They both knew that the only real danger was that Terry could go into a cardiac arrest en route but it seemed unlikely given how stable his cardiac rhythm was looking despite the changes happening with the heart attack and they were going to get Terry into the safety of the emergency department as soon as possible. They were already rolling the stretcher towards the door. These paramedics were just as capable as Emma of dealing with a cardiac arrest and, if she went in with the ambulance, how would she get home again?

Max was winding up the wires for the defibrillator. 'You go with Terry,' he told Jenny. 'We'll tidy up the mess we've made and then lock up. I'll leave the key in the usual place, yes?'

'Oh…thank you, Max. I can't tell you how grateful we are… You and your dad… Well, we're just blessed to have you in Upper Barnsley, that's what…'

'I'll call the hospital in a bit to find out what's happening.' Max had paused in his task to smile at Jenny. 'He's going to exactly where he needs to be,' he said gently. 'Try not to worry.'

Emma went with Jenny to see her climb into the front passenger seat of the ambulance, which had its lights flashing in the drift of snowflakes as it drove away. She went back inside to help Max tidy up, picking up packaging from the IV supplies and the plastic squares that had come off the ECG electrodes. He was rolling up the IV kit and slotting it back into place in the first-aid pack.

It was only then that Emma realised they were alone again for the first time since they had shared that astonishing kiss.

Since Max had pretty much admitted that he'd always fancied her. Since she had told him pretty much the same thing.

The silence was suddenly a little awkward.

'It's really snowing out there,' Emma finally said. 'I might have to put chains on my car to get into work in the morning.'

'They'll clear the roads fast.' Max zipped up the pocket that held the small oxygen tank in the kit.

'Should I have gone in with Terry, do you think?'

'He didn't need you.' Max's tone was reassuring. 'I know those paramedics and they're great. He'll be safely in the cath lab within an hour and I reckon he's going to be fine. It might muck up their Christmas plans but Terry will probably end up being a lot healthier than he's been for a long time.' He stood up. 'Besides... I need you.' He offered her the ghost of a wink. 'There's too much gear to carry.'

Emma's heart skipped a beat but her mouth was suddenly too dry to supply the obvious comment that he had managed to carry everything here by himself not so long ago. The look he was giving her was intense enough to make her quite sure that Max was not referring to any help with returning the clinic's gear. No... That look had made it feel as if Max was thinking about that kiss again. About what it might be like to do it again. To take it wherever it might lead—and they both knew exactly where that was. They were also about to head to a part of that huge house that was well away from the children and any threat of interruption. If Emma wanted to reinstate her resolution not to distract Max from his new responsibilities as a father figure by making herself available, this was quite probably her last chance.

But would it be such a bad thing if they both gave in to the simmering attraction that was on the point of boiling over? It wasn't as if it was going to change anything. In less than a couple of weeks, Emma could be almost anywhere in the world taking up a new locum position. She might never see Max again. How weird was this, that she was talking herself into being with a man she had steered well clear of years ago because he lived his life thinking along those same lines—that it was perfectly acceptable to give in to physical desire with no intention of it ever being anything more than that?

And if she didn't, Emma might never know if what she was imagining was true. That Max Cunningham could give her a night that she would remember for the rest of her life.

'I'll take the kit,' she said, turning away because if she kept eye contact with Max it might make her so nervous she would change her mind. 'It looks lighter than the defibrillator.'

They walked past the front door of the main part of the house.

'Looks like it's all quiet on the western front,' Max said.

It was a bit of a relief for Emma to find something new to talk about. They had already exhausted how thickly the snow was falling and whether Terry might already be out of the emergency department at the Royal and on his way to the catheter laboratory.

'I thought the clinic rooms were in the west wing. And they're around the corner.'

'True. But it wouldn't sound right saying it looks like it's all quiet on the southern front, would it?'

They turned the corner of the house. There were downstairs lights still on so it was easy enough to see where they were going. Emma could also see snow gathering on the ivy that scrambled over the old stones and even a curl of smoke coming from one of the many chimneys.

'It's a gorgeous house,' she said aloud. 'What a magic place to have grown up in.'

'It was,' Max agreed. 'But it was never the same after Mum died. I was glad to get away when I went to med school, to tell the truth. There were sad shadows everywhere and I don't think any of us knew how to shine a light to get rid of them. Andy got the closest. He set out to create a family of his own. To celebrate Christmas again.' Max shook his head as he opened the door of Upper Barnsley's general practice. 'That gave us a whole new level of sad stuff, what with the failure of his marriage and then his death and now three kids who are going to grow up without any parents.'

'They've got you.' Emma put the first-aid pack down in a corner of the waiting room. 'And I think they've got their grandpa now, as well. Did you see the way he was holding hands with Ben when we left the house? The way Pirate was right beside them? He's given them a bond, that little dog.'

'I think you might be right.' Max put the defibrillator back where it belonged on the bench. 'I hope so, anyway. I was old enough to help take care of Andy when Mum died but these kids really need him and that might well be enough to bring him out of his shell. He's been hiding for far too long.'

Emma opened her mouth. She had been about to say that James wasn't the only one who'd been hiding. That maybe Max himself needed to learn to trust in love again—enough to be able to commit to making that love a significant part of his life. That loving his nieces and nephew would be a very good place to start.

But that was something he needed to discover for himself, wasn't it?

'It's not easy,' she said, instead. 'Letting anybody into your heart when you know how hard it is to lose a person you care about that much. I think your mum must have been a wonderful person. She certainly loved Christmas. I can't believe how many decorations we've put out today.'

'You know what?' Max was smiling at Emma. 'I love seeing them out again. There are happy memories to be found now and they're even stronger than the sad ones. We kept the smallest decorations that we could find and put them on that little tree that Ben was carrying with him when he arrived. I put it in their bedroom.'

Emma's smile was meant to be encouraging

but she knew it was wobbling a bit. 'That was a sweet thing to do. That tree was special.'

'I want to remember what Christmas used to be like when I was a kid,' Max added. 'I want Ben and Tilly to feel like that too. And Alice, when she's old enough. I want to get that blue bike for Ben and have it waiting under the Christmas tree for him so that he comes down and just knows that the magic is real. That Father Christmas is real and got his letter—the way I did when I got my first bike.'

Emma's smile felt even more wobbly, now. Maybe Max was already well on the way to opening his heart again. It was quite possible that he didn't trust the idea of marriage after his father was so devastated by his wife's death and then his brother by his broken marriage, but if he changed his mind he wouldn't have any trouble finding someone who would want to love him back. Someone who could end up being a mother to those three children and give him the kind of family he'd once had himself? He deserved that.

'I know he'll find out the truth one day but that can wait, can't it? He can have a bit of time to believe in magic?'

Max had stepped closer to Emma as he was speaking and now he was close enough to touch her face. To let his fingers and thumb slide so gently down her cheeks and then to cup her chin softly as he bent his head ready to cover her lips with his own.

'This is magic I can still believe in…' he said softly.

Emma's weight was on her toes and she tilted her body to touch his as she returned that kiss and felt his hands move to trace the shape of her shoulders and slip between them to touch her breasts. Emma could only gasp at the spear of sensation that coursed through her body and the movement of Max's hands stilled instantly, as though he was afraid she didn't want this.

Which couldn't be further from the truth. Emma had never wanted anything in her life as much as she wanted the escape of sinking into a timeless bliss that would make anything else in the world irrelevant. She wanted that magic…

'Don't stop,' she whispered, lifting her face to kiss Max again. 'Please don't stop…'

CHAPTER NINE

HAD SHE REALLY believed that giving in to this overwhelmingly powerful attraction between herself and Max Cunningham meant nothing would actually change?

How wrong had Emma been?

Everything had changed.

She couldn't stop thinking about it. About every touch of his hands. Every kiss, from those so tender they could bring tears to her eyes to ones so passionate they made the world tilt on its axis. Almost falling asleep cradled in his arms in the aftermath of their lovemaking, feeling the steady thump of his heartbeat beneath her cheek, until he'd reminded her gently that they needed to leave this secret room above the practice clinic. He had to be in the main part of the house in case the children needed him during the night.

She'd lain awake in her own room for a long time, reliving every moment of their time together. She'd been absolutely right about one thing—she'd experienced something she would never, ever forget. Something which had made her feel as if she was stepping out of ordinary life into a place that felt very different. A bright place where colours were more intense, where food tasted better and something as simple as the scent of a pine tree in the house was special. A place where laughter was the most beautiful sound in the world, the excitement of watching snow falling thickly was so strong it took her back to her own childhood and even the chore of getting the chains onto her tyres so that she could get to work this afternoon was not nearly as tiresome as it could have been.

It was a place that Emma finally recognised, even though she'd never experienced it to this kind of level.

At first, it was a surprise to be getting frequent text messages from Max as she attended to one task after another during a busy Christmas Eve shift in an emergency department. She received images of Ben and Tilly standing in the snow in their gumboots, with carrots in their hands that they were going to leave out for the reindeer, when she snatched a few minutes to go and visit Terry on the cardiology ward and catch up with the great news that he'd received several stents in his coronary arteries, fast enough for the damage from his heart attack to be minimal.

There was one of Pirate with some tinsel tied to his collar, being cuddled by Ben, that arrived in the minute or two between Emma sending an eighty-year-old woman off to X-ray, knowing that she'd broken her hip when she'd slipped in the snow on her front step, and going to stitch up a nasty laceration on a young man whose Christmas party had gone seriously awry.

The best thing about that image was that the small boy was sitting on his grandfather's knee when the picture had been taken and Emma had to blink away a tear, knowing that at least one of the barriers in the Cunningham household was beginning to crumble.

The one Max had sent much later, when the

children must have been settled in bed and he'd been able to sneak back to the rooms above the clinic where the gifts had been hidden had broken her focus quite noticeably.

Was Max remembering what had happened in that room last night in as much detail as she was? His attempt to wrap Ben's bicycle in Christmas paper did make her laugh, though, and that eased the emotional tension that she could feel building.

She texted back.

Great effort. Just leave it like that with the pedals and handlebars sticking out. It's not as if Ben's not going to recognise it instantly— he asked Father Christmas for it, didn't he?

Things got really busy in the department as it got closer to midnight. A stabbing victim from a pub brawl meant that Emma was tied up in Resus for a long, difficult time. When they'd finally sent the critically ill patient up to Theatre, finding the selfie Max had taken wearing the sparkly tiara that was part of Tilly's fairy supplies had made her smile rather than laugh.

She'd spent long seconds just staring at the face that filled her screen and remembering what it had been like to have those beautiful, dark blue eyes staring into her own when they'd been as physically close as it was possible for two people to be.

She texted back again.

Wish I was there. Looks much more fun than being here.

Max's text came instantly.

Wish you were here too. More than you can imagine.

Oh…she could actually imagine it only too well if it was anything like she was feeling and it was when the physical tingling in her body morphed into a longing that was intense enough to steal her breath that Emma finally recognised what was going on.

She was in love with Max Cunningham.

It wasn't just that he'd given her the best sex

she'd ever experienced in her life. The sex could only have been that amazing thanks to the connection that had already been there. Because the trust had already been there between them—a mix of familiarity from knowing each other long ago, respecting each other in both professional and personal capacities and shared experiences of dealing with tough things in life. Because there was a possibility that she'd always been a little bit in love with Max, she'd just never let herself go there because she didn't belong in his kind of world.

She still didn't belong here with a new family just trying to glue themselves together, so being in love with this man was only ever going to be a problem—especially when it made her feel as if she wanted to stay in exactly this part of the world and not move on to a new position in the very near future. When it made her feel as if she could quite easily open her heart to the generations of Cunninghams on either side of Max and have an instant family of a size that her Italian relatives would approve of heartily.

Even if Max wasn't taking the first steps to try and piece together a new lifestyle when his old one had exploded around him, he had never wanted the same things in life as Emma. She could understand why he'd thrown around that catchphrase of being here for a good time not a long time, given the early tragedy in his life, but the truth of the matter was that Max was never going to give his heart away. Not in the way that Emma could with the person she might want to choose to spend the rest of her life with.

Oh, he would love the children who had unexpectedly come to share his life—he already did—and he would take the best care of them and of his father, but that was far more responsibility than he'd ever planned to take on and, eventually, he would sort out the current chaos around him. He would employ a full-time housekeeper and nanny and be able to come back to his job in the Royal's emergency department in the very near future. He would get his apartment repaired and most likely keep it on, despite living in the manor house, because it would be the perfect place to find private time with the women who would always be eager to be chosen even though they knew—like Emma did—that it might only be a one-off night to treasure. He might be even less likely to consider a long-term relationship—not only because he'd seen his brother's marriage end in misery—but because it wouldn't be fair on three children who'd already experienced far too much disruption in their lives.

Being in love with Max was her problem, Emma realised, and it would be far better if nobody else knew anything about it. Max probably wouldn't notice, especially tomorrow when it was Christmas Day and would be all about the children. Or make that today, she thought, as she checked her watch to find midnight had come and gone a while back. That meant she was closer to being able to escape before Max had the chance to notice anything different about her. She'd only ever promised to stay long enough to help create a magical Christmas Day for Ben and Tilly and Alice. Only one more day and that had started already. She had a day off rostered for Boxing Day and Emma could use that to find somewhere else to stay. There was only one more week after that until New Year's Day and that was when Max had told her the new nanny was due to arrive.

So that would be that. Maybe they'd stay in touch and Max would send a Christmas card every year with photos tracking the changes as the children grew up. It was just as well you could send digital cards now because goodness only knew where in the world Emma was likely to be.

She tapped the screen to enlarge the photo of Max in the tiara again. To soak in the expression in his eyes and that smile.

'Dr Moretti? We've got a Status One patient arriving by ambulance. Electrocution from faulty Christmas tree lights but someone had started CPR before the paramedics got there and they've got a perfusing rhythm again. ETA two minutes…'

'Resus One clear?'

'Yes.'

'Activate the trauma team, please. And get whoever's on call in Cardiology down here stat.'

Her phone slipped back into the pocket of her scrub suit. Goodness also only knew when she'd get the next chance to check on the progress of the gift wrapping and that was a good thing.

Emma needed to try and step back.

To keep things under control so that nobody got hurt, including herself. It was Christmas Day and she was going to play her part to make it as perfect as possible for the Cunningham family and as little as possible about herself. It was a strategy that had worked for years now.

She was good at it.

She was also good at her job and right now she had the challenge of dealing with a post-cardiac arrest due to electrocution. This person wasn't going to die in the early hours of Christmas Day. Not if Emma Moretti could do anything to change that.

* * *

Max was the first person awake in the Cunningham household on Christmas Day which surprised him, not only because he'd been up in the night with Alice and should have been tired enough to sleep through all but a major disturbance but because he remembered the way he and Andy would get up while it was still dark and tiptoe past their parents' bedroom to go downstairs and see if the Christmas magic had happened again this year.

He could hear soft snuffles coming from the cot in the corner of his room but that wasn't the sound which had woken him. It was the light tapping that was coming from the hallway beyond his open door—the sound of a small dog's toenails on the wooden floorboards on either side of the carpet runner. So he wasn't really the first person awake, after all. He had to smile when he heard Ben's whisper that was even more audible than Pirate's toenails.

'Shh, Pirate... Don't wake up Uncle Max. Let's find Grandpa first because we have to have a Christmas cuddle… It's one of the rules…'

Oh… Max knew who he'd like to be having a Christmas cuddle with right now. How horrified would Emma be if she knew just how much she'd been on his mind since they'd made love in the early hours of Christmas Eve? He wanted to do that again. As soon as possible.

As often as possible.

For the rest of his life…

Good grief… Max was properly awake now, that was for sure. How on earth had that thought surfaced again? He'd already sorted things out in his head after he'd had that disturbing glimpse through his personal barriers and thought, for a heartbeat, that he wanted the kind of partnership his parents had had when they'd created their family. That Andy had thought he'd found with the woman he'd fallen so deeply in love with.

Was that what was happening here?

Was Max falling in love with Emma?

No. He didn't do 'falling in love'. Never had, never would allow himself to take that kind of risk. It was what women did with him and it had always been enough to make him end things rapidly. Falling in love was a magic you only believed in until you learned that the truth could be very different and he'd learned that at a very young age. It was like Christmas magic, until you discovered Father Christmas didn't actually exist. Ben still believed. And Max wanted to be there when the little boy went downstairs and saw his bike under the Christmas tree because he wanted to remember what it had been like for himself all those years ago. He wanted to feel *that* magic, just for a heartbeat.

Max pushed the bedclothes away and reached for his clothes. A pair of jeans and a tee shirt and an extra warm woollen jersey because he could feel that the central heating was already struggling this morning. There was also that odd feeling of silence that only came when the world was blanketed thickly enough by snow. Would Emma make it home safely after her shift ended this morning?

And there she was again. In his head.

In his heart, as well, judging by the squeezing sensation he was aware of in his chest even though he knew that the heart was not an organ that was capable of either thinking or feeling. That was disturbing too. A kind of magic all of its own.

He had to get a handle on this. He wanted this Christmas Day to be special for Emma so that she could get on with her life and find joy again. He wanted it to be special for Ben and Tilly and Alice. For his father as well, because it might be a struggle for him to cope today. How had he reacted to a small boy and a dog climbing into his bed for a pre-dawn Christmas cuddle? Taking the handset of the baby monitor with him, Max left his room to go and find out.

'I got a *bike*, Emma. A blue bike—just like I asked for...'

'Oh...that's amazing, Ben.' It was impossible not to return the happy smile that Emma had received full blast when she'd finally arrived back after a shift that had gone overtime.

'Did he make it?' Max came out of the

drawing room a few seconds after Ben had run to meet Emma at the front door. He had Tilly perched on one hip and she was in her full fairy outfit with the tutu and wings and tiara. 'The Christmas lights guy?'

'He was sitting up and talking by the time I left. He's not going to get home for his Christmas dinner but I don't think his family's too bothered.'

'I'm sure they're just delighted he's still alive.' Max nodded. He was holding Emma's gaze and he looked delighted as well, she thought. Because of a successful case in his department, or was he as pleased to see her as she was to see him again? The warmth that was coursing through her body made it urgent to get her coat and hat and scarf off and hang them on the hooks.

'I'm a fairy,' Tilly told her.

'I can see that, sweetheart. You're the prettiest fairy I've ever seen.' Emma pulled in a deep breath. 'Something smells gorgeous,' she added.

'That'll be what Maggie and Ruth are cooking up. Turkey and bread sauce and Brussels sprouts and roasted potatoes—the whole nine yards. Pigs in blankets for Ben too. They got here before it started snowing again, which is lucky. How did you find the roads?'

'A bit dodgy around here. They must have cleared them this morning but it was just as well I had chains on. It's still snowing hard.'

'But I want to ride my bike,' Ben said sadly.

'How 'bout we make a snowman instead?' Max suggested. 'After we've had our dinner? It might have stopped snowing by then. Otherwise, we might be stuck inside for a while yet.' He gave Emma just the ghost of a wink. 'We'll have to think of other ways to entertain ourselves if that happens.'

Emma had to drag her gaze away from Max. That gleam in his eyes told her exactly what kind of entertainment he had in mind and it felt wrong to be thinking about that in the presence of two small children.

'I'll go and see if Maggie and Ruth need my help in the kitchen,' she said.

'Come in by the fire for a minute first. Dad

insisted on opening some champagne,' Max told her. 'There's a glass with your name on it.'

'It's a rule,' Ben told her. 'Grandpa said it was one of Nana's rules but it's only for grown-ups. Come on, Emma. Come and see our new toys. And there's new stories too…'

'Yes…' Max was smiling. 'Come on, Emma. We're having a very special Christmas but we've all been waiting for you to come and share it.'

The floor of the drawing room was littered with crumpled wrapping paper. Alice was asleep in her pram near James's chair and Pirate was lying at his feet chewing happily on a dog treat bone. The lights on the Christmas tree were sparkling and the fire was glowing. Emma watched Tilly slide to the floor from her uncle's arms so he could pour the champagne and then she went to climb onto her grandfather's lap as if it was the most natural thing in the world to do. Ben picked up a picture book from a pile and handed it to James, curling up on the floor beside Pirate

as the most senior member of the Cunningham family started reading the story.

She was already a little spaced out from
working a night shift and it felt as if she had
stepped into a Christmas card scene so she
sipped her celebratory drink cautiously as
Max came to stand beside her near the fire.
This was exactly what she'd imagined when
she'd told Max how important this Christmas
was to these children and the opportunity it
was providing for them to bond as a family.
This was perfect and it was a pleasure to be
a part of it and to be watching it happening.
And, according to Max, even better news was
waiting in the wings.

'Do you remember that I told you that
Maggie's daughter Ruth is an infant school
teacher?'

Emma nodded. 'You said she was wonderful with the children.'

She'd been looking after them when Max
had taken Emma up to the attic to find the
boxes of decorations. It seemed a long time
ago already that James had been so upset to
see them being used again. He had a grand-

child on his lap right now and another one leaning on his leg and he looked like a man who'd had his heart well and truly stolen.

'She is. And Maggie says she wants to come and live in Upper Barnsley so that her mum can help after the baby's born. They've cooked up a plan between them that Ruth could be our nanny and Maggie can stay on as housekeeper as well as helping to look after Ruth's baby. It sounds like a good plan, doesn't it?'

Emma's head was definitely spinning now. 'It sounds perfect,' she agreed. 'You'll be able to go back to work. You might not even need to wait until the New Year?'

Which meant that Emma wouldn't be needed as a locum any longer. If she left the manor house tomorrow, she might never see it again. Or see James or the children or Max again and that simply felt...wrong...

Very wrong...

'Dr Cunningham?'

'What is it, Maggie?' Both Max and James turned towards the anxious voice at the door, where their housekeeper was wiping her hands on her apron.

'Would one of you have a minute? Ruth isn't feeling terribly well.'

Emma put her glass on the mantelpiece, turning back swiftly, but Max was well ahead of her as she left the room. Glancing over her shoulder just before she pulled the door closed behind her, Emma could see that Ben was climbing up to join his grandad and Tilly in the roomy leather chair and that James was nodding, quite prepared to take responsibility for the children.

A short time later Emma wished she had stayed where she was and sent James in to assist his son. It had taken Max only minutes to find out why Ruth had started feeling so awful she had gone to lie down on the old couch at one end of the huge kitchen.

'You're in labour,' he told her. 'You're far enough along for it to be safe for the baby but it looks as though you might already be close to the end of the first stage and that means that it's happening very fast. I'm not happy to try driving you to hospital and risk you having your baby on the side of the road. I'll call for an ambulance but there's no guarantee it'll get here in time with the amount of snow on the road.'

The way Emma's head was spinning now had nothing to do with fatigue or the sip of champagne she'd had. This was more like an adrenaline overload. A fight or flight response and all she wanted to do was flee.

Another baby was about to be born on Christmas Day?

No…no, no, no…

She couldn't do this.

But now Max was standing in front of her and his gaze was telling her that she *could* do this. That she had to because he needed her to.

'You know where the kit is in the clinic,' he said. 'Could you go and get it, please? There's an obstetric pack right beside the drug cupboard too. Maggie's got a key. She'll go with you to get what we need, but we need it fast.'

Getting out of this room was good. Getting out fast was even better.

Emma turned and ran.

CHAPTER TEN

THIS HAD TO be the most unusual management of an emergency that Max had ever been in charge of. Here he was, in the kitchen of his childhood home, the aromas of a traditional Christmas dinner beginning to fill the room, and he was about to help a new baby into the world.

An ambulance was on its way to the house but he was pretty sure it was not going to arrive in time for the crew to be present at the birth of this baby. He hoped that was the case, anyway, because a long delay at this stage of a delivery could mean there were complications so a smooth transition and fast birth were preferable.

Ruth must have been having contractions for some time. She'd told Max that she'd put her discomfort down to an increase in the backache she'd been aware of for a couple of days, due to being on her feet since early this morning helping her mother cook the Christmas dinner they'd all been planning to share. By the time Emma and Maggie had come back into the room with the kit and Max had pulled gloves on, he could feel the bulge in Ruth's perineum that meant that crowning of the baby's head was imminent.

Ruth wasn't his only patient here. There was a baby that was about to come into the world a lot faster than usual, and that was a worry due to increased risks of haemorrhage or tearing for the mother and aspiration of amniotic fluid for the baby, or infection due to a less than sterile environment for the birth.

'Grab some clean towels, Maggie. We'll put some under Ruth right away. I'm surprised her waters haven't broken already.'

Maggie was pale but composed. 'I'll be right back... Oh, my...that's the bread sauce boiling over. I thought I could smell something burning...'

Max wasn't the only doctor here either.

Emma had opened the kit. She had also put gloves on and she was unrolling the IV pack. She knew that IV access was a priority. Not for intravenous pain relief because it was probably already too late for that, but they might need to be able to give fluids if Ruth started losing too much blood.

But Emma was even paler than Maggie. She was doing what she needed to do but Max could feel how difficult this was for her. He could almost see the pressure that she was fighting against.

And he understood completely just how hard this had to be for Emma.

Her own baby had been born on Christmas Day and, while Holly had been born alive, it had only been a short time later that Emma had lost her daughter. This had to be taking her back to the pain, both physical and emotional, and Max could feel a piece of his own heart tearing.

It was unbearable to see Emma in such pain. He wished he could have protected her from this but he hadn't been able to. The urge to offer comfort now was so strong it had the potential to interfere with what he needed to focus on, and it was in that split second that Max realised just how important Emma was to him.

He wasn't in danger of falling in love with this woman.

It had already happened. In the space of only a few days, with his world as he knew it crumbling into chaos around him, he had found a human rock who had anchored him. Who had shown him a future that he could embrace. Someone who had touched him on levels he'd never experienced before and he knew he could never find with anyone else. Max was a better man for having had Emma Moretti in his life for only a matter of days. Already, he couldn't imagine his life without her in it.

So he was feeling her pain but he knew that, somehow, she had to face it or she would never be able to move on and embrace a future of her own—whether it was with him or not. And, because he loved her, he had to help her.

The thoughts flashed through his brain as

more of an awareness than any conscious analysis. His focus had to be fully on his patients and, as Maggie arrived with soft, clean towels that were put in place merely seconds before Ruth's waters broke, Max only had a heartbeat to catch Emma's gaze. To try and let her know that he understood. That he was going to do whatever it took to make sure that Emma could cope. That everything was going to be okay.

You've got this...

His message was silent but he knew that it had been received because he could sense the contact. As if she had accepted an outstretched hand. As if his strength was welcome.

It seemed as if every new situation that Emma saw Max dealing with increased her respect for this man and filled her heart with a mix of emotions that felt limitless.

Like how proud she was of his abilities. Like how much she loved how gentle he was trying to be but how uncompromising he was in doing what needed to be done, like cradling the back of the baby's head as it appeared and putting pressure on it to prevent an explosive delivery. His hand looked huge as he supported the tiny head as the forehead and then the face and finally the chin and neck were delivered and then helping to deliver each shoulder by careful downward pressure for the first and upward for the second.

'You're doing great, Ruth. Almost there...'

Dear Lord, it was hard to try and keep a totally professional focus, here. Emma could feel the pain of every contraction Ruth was having and she could remember exactly what it felt like to have the rest of a baby's body slither out after the shoulders were delivered. That moment, suspended in time, when you were listening for the first cry of your child. That moment had been so much worse for Emma, because she'd known there was a very good chance she might never hear a first cry but oh...she could have wished to have had Max present at the birth of her own baby.

The way he'd looked at her, only minutes ago, when she'd returned to try and assist him in this unexpected and precipitous birth. As if he understood exactly how hard this might be for her but he had complete confidence that his admiration for how she could cope with difficult things was not misplaced. It felt like the way he'd looked at her when she'd first told him the tragic story of Holly's birth. As though the threads of connection between them were becoming so strong they could be trusted to take any amount of weight.

But perhaps he was wrong…

It was that first cry of Ruth's baby that tipped the balance. It took Emma straight back to that delivery room five years ago. To the mindset that she could cope because she'd known what was going to happen but…but then *she'd* been wrong. It might have looked to others as if she'd coped and carried on coping but that was only because she'd been hiding. She'd run away emotionally and built protective walls that had just come crashing down with the single warbling cry of a newborn baby.

'I'm…sorry…' The words came out as a whisper as Emma pushed herself to her feet. 'I… I have to go…'

* * *

Where was she?

It was nearly an hour later that Max could finally focus on what had been an increasingly urgent concern. Emma hadn't been seen since she'd fled the kitchen after the birth of Ruth's baby. He hadn't been able to go after her then, of course. His responsibilities lay with caring for his patients, even though it appeared that everything had gone as well as he could have hoped it would. The baby's Apgar score was good at one minute and perfect at ten minutes. Ruth experienced only minor blood loss and her placenta was delivered without any problem. When the ambulance arrived, along with a police escort and a snow plough waiting at the end of the driveway, Ruth's tiny son was already nursing well and a proud grandmother was ready to accompany them to hospital.

'Just to be on the safe side,' Max told Maggie. 'I'm sure they'll have you all back home by this afternoon.'

'I can't thank you enough.' Maggie brushed back tears. 'I've just helped Dr Cunningham to change Alice's nappy and given him a bottle for her but I think your Christmas dinner might be a bit ruined. The turkey and potatoes have been in the oven a bit too long and that bread sauce is inedible.'

'It doesn't matter.' Max was smiling. 'It was your Christmas dinner as well and I'm sure you're not worried about missing it.'

'You could heat up the pigs in blankets for Ben. And there's red jelly in the fridge. I'm sorry, Max. I wanted to help make this Christmas perfect for all of you.'

'We'll be fine. You go and take care of your family, Maggie. I can take care of mine.'

'But where's Emma?'

'That's what I'm about to find out.'

He checked the drawing room but hadn't expected to find her with his father and the children. That heartbreaking look in her eyes when she'd heard Ruth's baby cry for the first time had told him that she was facing a ghost she thought she had to grapple with alone.

But she was wrong.

She needed him. Or maybe it was that Max needed to be with her.

He checked her room but it was empty.

He went outside into a world that was silent and white, with a fresh burst of fat snowflakes drifting slowly down to cover the tyre tracks of the emergency vehicles that were now long gone. The biting cold nipped at his skin and Max stared towards the woods on either side of the driveway but then he shook his head. Emma was far from stupid and she hadn't been dressed for being outdoors. Besides, there were no footprints in the snow leading towards the woods.

There were, however, footprints that led around the corner of the house. A lot of prints, but was that because they'd been made when Maggie and Emma had gone to fetch the medical gear he'd asked for? With the new snow falling, it was hard to tell whether there were any more recent tracks but Max kept following them.

Because he was remembering walking this way with Emma when they'd brought the emergency kit back from the neighbours' house and where they'd ended up, later that night. He was remembering not the mind-blowing sexual encounter but what it had been like afterwards. When he'd held Emma in his arms, skin to skin. Heartbeat to heartbeat. How it had felt like the most perfect place in the world to ever be.

If he was in pain, or scared, or he simply needed comfort, that would be the place he would want to be, wouldn't it? In Emma's arms. But, if that hadn't been possible, he might well have chosen the next best thing— to be in the place that he *had* once been in Emma's arms, so that he could imagine that comfort and wrap himself in it like the warmest blanket on a day exactly like today.

Max let himself into the clinic and then headed for the stairs to the room above.

Those agonised tears had finally stopped a while back.

Emma had curled herself into the smallest ball and pulled the old eiderdown that had been rolled up on the end of this antique brass bed over herself. She'd heard someone coming up the stairs from the clinic rooms and she'd known that it would be Max, because he was the only person who would know that she knew about the existence of this room, but she was too exhausted to move. So utterly drained she thought she might never be able to move again.

He didn't say anything when he came into this room. What he did do was to lie down on the other side of the bed, beneath the eiderdown and behind Emma, to not only take her into his arms but to wrap his whole body around hers. His warmth seeped into her skin with far more effect than the feather-filled cover over them both and she could feel his heartbeat against her back. A steady ticking that was an affirmation of life.

Of caring…

It felt like love…

His words, when they came, were soft against her ear.

'I know it hurts. I've got you. It's going to be okay…'

Emma's words were shaky. 'But it's not. I thought it was. I want it to be but… I'm scared. I thought I had it sorted but I didn't really. I've been hiding—all this time. It broke me, Max, hearing that cry. I would give anything to hear another baby of mine cry, but how could I ever go through that again when I know how much it can hurt?'

'You can't hide for ever.' Max was stroking Emma's hair. 'Well, you can, but I hope you don't. You have so much love to give, Em. So much love that others will want to give you. If you keep hiding, they won't be able to find you and you'll miss out on both giving and receiving that love, and how sad would that be?'

Emma turned in his arms so that she could press her face against the reassuring beat of his heart.

'Nobody's trying to find me,' she said quietly. 'I've made sure I never stay in one place long enough for that to happen.'

'It doesn't always take a long time.' Emma felt Max's lips press against the top of her head. 'I've found you—and I wasn't even looking.'

Emma's breath caught.

'I didn't want to look,' he continued softly. 'Because I guess I was hiding too. Even when it was right in front of my eyes I couldn't see it properly. Like that night when you were making stars with Ben and Tilly and I was feeding Alice and I felt like...like we were...'

'A family?' Emma whispered into the silence. 'I know. I felt like that too, when we were decorating the tree. Until your dad got so upset. Until I remembered how much safer it was to step back. To hide...'

'I didn't believe in Christmas,' Max said. 'I knew the magic wasn't real. That it had died when Mum had gone but, you know what?'

Emma pulled back just far enough to be able to see Max's face. 'What?'

'You've made me believe in a different sort of Christmas. And a different sort of magic. Not the sort when you believe someone comes down the chimney and gives you the bike you've wanted for so long, but it's still magic. The family kind. My dad's probably still sitting in front of the fire, playing with his grandkids or reading them another story. Maybe he's gone into the kitchen to heat up those pigs in blankets for Ben or maybe they've just gone straight for the red jelly. But what he's really doing is letting those kids into his heart and that means he's going to start living again. Really living…and that's magic, isn't it?'

Emma could feel her eyes filling. A single tear escaping to trickle down her cheek. 'It is… It's real magic. Like love…'

'I tried to make you stay with us because I knew that couldn't have happened without you. We need you, Em. We all need you but I need you most of all. I love you, Emma Moretti. I'm *in* love with you and I never thought I'd ever say that to anyone because I didn't believe in that magic either and I know that you're the only woman in the world that could make me believe in it. I want you to stay for the rest of this Christmas. And next Christmas. For every Christmas to come for as long as I live.'

Tears were falling freely now. Max had come out of the place he'd been hiding in for most of his life. He was risking his heart. For the children who had come into his life but for *her* as well.

Could Emma be that brave?

'I love you too, Max. I need you. I want to stop hiding but I can only do that because you make me feel a lot braver than I really am. I want to be here for every one of those Christmases and...'

And then Emma had to stop talking because Max was kissing her. There were tears mixed into that kiss. A bit of laughter too and a great deal of love. And then, with their arms wrapped tightly around each other, they went back into the house.

To the family that was waiting for them both.

EPILOGUE

Two years later...

IT WAS JUST as well that the Cunninghams' manor house had so many bedrooms because it seemed like the house had to cater for more visitors every year.

'Sorry, Maggie...' Emma eyed the huge pile of tiny sausages that were having strips of bacon wrapped around them and secured with toothpicks. 'I'll have to start limiting how many of my relatives come over here from Italy for Christmas before it gets to be way too much work.' She went to the sink to wash her hands so that she could start helping with the preparations. 'I wonder what they'll think of these pigs in blankets? I tried translating the idea but my *nonna* looked very dubious.'

Maggie laughed. 'I'm sure she'll love them.

And I love how full the house is and how many children we've got running around. I loved that we had the feast of the seven fishes last night too. And that your mum brought your family's gorgeous nativity scene. Ruth's loving it all as well. She was so impressed with your star making class yesterday.'

It was Emma's turn to laugh. 'We've got so many wonky stars now, I think I'll have to make a string to put across the ceiling next year or we won't have room for all the other decorations on our tree.'

'Ruth will help with that. She says her job is like she's running her own little school and the best bit is that she gets to take her wee Joseph to work with her.'

Emma peered out of the window as she dried her hands. Ruth's two-year-old son was as much a part of the crowd of excited children outside as her Italian nieces and nephews.

'Ben's got him in the wheelbarrow,' she said. 'Along with Alice. I hope he can cope with both of them. They're a bit like twins, aren't they? There's six months between them but they're inseparable.'

'Maybe it's because we celebrate Joe's half-birthday so it doesn't get lost in Christmas. Tilly is convinced they're both the same age.' Maggie started a new row of the wrapped sausages on the oven tray. 'Is Ruth out there supervising?'

'Ruth *and* Max.' Emma was still looking out of the window. 'They look like they've got everything under control for the moment. Pirate's out there too but he's probably as eager as everyone to get back inside. What made us decide that the kids could only open their stockings before breakfast and we'd do the gifts under the tree before dinner?'

'Oh…that reminds me. Ben was worried about where his little tree was. You know, the one he brought with him when he first arrived and that we save all the tiniest decorations for?'

'I put it up high to keep it safe,' Emma said. 'The toddlers were getting into everything. It's a circus around here at the moment.'

But she was loving it. Every moment of

it. Because every day brought so much love, along with something new and special into her life. Today one of the special things was that this was the first Christmas for the newest member of the Cunningham clan. Emma forgot that she was about to help Maggie create the army of pigs in blankets. Instead, she walked towards the pram parked on the other side of the Aga stove, to gaze at her four-month-old daughter. Hannah had been named after her paternal grandmother and was currently dressed in the cutest stretchy suit ever—a tiny green elf outfit, right down to booties with curly toes and a green and red hat. She was awake in her pram but not crying and when she saw her mother her little face lit up with the widest smile and she held out her arms to be picked up.

The kitchen door opened as Emma gathered her baby into her arms. Max's face lit up with the same kind of joy as Hannah's and he went straight to his wife and daughter to wrap his arms around both of them.

'Where's Dad?' he asked Maggie.

Maggie's face softened with a smile that

made Max and Emma share a knowing glance. They suspected that something might be going on there and this looked like another clue.

'He's upstairs, putting on that Santa suit so he can distribute the presents. Shall I go and see if he's ready?'

'Good idea.' Max nodded. 'I'm not sure how long Ruth will manage to keep the troops out of the way. I don't think we'll be getting any kind of white Christmas this year but it's pretty cold out there.'

He waited until Maggie had gone out of the kitchen before he bent his head to kiss Emma—a slow, tender kiss that tapped into everything she loved so much about her husband and about their life together which was only getting better with every passing month. How had they not known, when they'd first met all those years ago, that they were so perfect for each other? That they could meet every challenge in life as long as they faced it together?

'Champagne?' he asked. 'I do believe it's one of those Christmas rules.'

'After the presents.' She smiled. 'As the other half of Upper Barnsley's general practice, I think I have a duty to cover any calls until your dad has changed out of his Santa suit.'

'I guess I'll wait too, then—so we can share that first toast to a happy Christmas.'

'It's already happy.' Emma smiled up at Max. 'I don't think it could be any happier.'

Except it could.

The kitchen door opened again and a stream of small children came rushing in.

'Mummy… Daddy…' Six-year-old Tilly was bursting with excitement. 'You've got to come… *Father Christmas* is here…'

Ben was by her side. He and Max exchanged a grin and Emma knew what that was about. As the oldest child, Ben was now in on the secret—that it was the family that made the magic happen at Christmas time but that was fine by him. He knew how important a part of this family he was and he was going to help make that magic happen from now on.

This Christmas was going to be the best yet.

Until next time, of course…

* * * * *

LET'S TALK
Romance

For exclusive extracts, competitions
and special offers, find us online:

- facebook.com/millsandboon
- @millsandboonuk
- @millsandboon

Or get in touch on 0844 844 1351*

For all the latest titles coming soon,
visit millsandboon.co.uk/nextmonth

Want even more
ROMANCE?

Join our bookclub today!